DATE DUE

MAR 0 1 2013		
MAR 1 4 2013		
APR 0 9 2013		
	OCT 2 0 2015	
OCT 1 1 2016		

H.I.V.E.

ROGUE

OTHER BOOKS BY MARK WALDEN

H.I.V.E.

ROGUE

MARK WALDEN

SIMON & SCHUSTER BOOKS FOR YOUNG READERS

NEW YORK LONDON TORONTO SYDNEY

SIMON & SCHUSTER BOOKS FOR YOUNG READERS
An imprint of Simon & Schuster Children's Publishing Division
1230 Avenue of the Americas, New York, New York 10020
Originally published in Great Britain in 2010 by Bloomsbury Publishing Plc
First U.S. edition September 2011
SIMON & SCHUSTER BOOKS FOR YOUNG READERS is a trademark
of Simon & Schuster, Inc.
For information about special discounts for bulk purchases, please contact Simon &
Schuster Special Sales at 1-866-506-1949 or business@simonandschuster.com.
The Simon & Schuster Speakers Bureau can bring authors to your live event. For more
information or to book an event, contact the Simon & Schuster Speakers Bureau at
1-866-248-3049 or visit our website at www.simonspeakers.com.
The text for this book is set in Goudy.
Manufactured in the United States of America
0112 FFG
2 4 6 8 10 9 7 5 3
CIP data for this book is available from the Library of Congress.
ISBN 978-1-4424-2187-5
ISBN 978-1-4424-1372-6 (eBook)

For Fred

H.I.V.E.

ROGUE

chapter one

Dr. Charles Morley hurried over to his workstation and reviewed the data scrolling past on the display. He swallowed nervously. Glancing across the large laboratory to the fluid-filled tank on the platform in the middle of the room, he couldn't help but notice that the other scientists gathered around it wore expressions of nervous fear that were a close match for his own. He continued to stare at the numbers on the screen and felt a wave of relief as he realized that the data was demonstrating exactly the results that they had been hoping for. They had only minutes before the man who had funded the project arrived for his regular inspection and all present were familiar with his intolerance of failure. The small intercom unit mounted on the wall nearby bleeped suddenly, and Dr. Morley hurried over to it and hit the button.

"Yes?" he asked impatiently.

"Dr. Morley?" the voice at the other end replied.

"Yes, what is it?" Morley snapped.

"You asked to be informed when our guest arrived," the voice said. "He's on his way down to you now."

"Th-thank you," Morley replied, feeling his throat go dry. He stepped away from the intercom and glanced toward the doors at the far end of the laboratory. "Ladies and gentlemen," he announced, "our client is on his way down. Please ensure that all relevant data is available for immediate review."

Barely a minute later the air lock doors that sealed off the laboratory hissed open, and a tall man with snow-white hair and an immaculately tailored suit walked into the room. His face betrayed no hint of emotion as he slowly surveyed the feverish activity around the room. None of them knew the man's real name—to them he was known simply as "the client." Whoever he was, he wielded an enormous amount of power. Enough to construct a facility like this in complete secrecy and to staff it with some of the best and brightest minds in their respective fields of expertise that money could buy. The man walked toward Morley, his cold blue eyes seeming to take in everything that was going on in the room with just a few quick glances.

"Report," the man said, ignoring Morley's offered hand-shake.

"We've made excellent progress with the latest subject," Morley replied, quickly lowering his outstretched hand. "All our tests indicate that the procedure has been a complete success."

"Indeed," the man said. "I have reviewed your latest data and your results seem promising. I assume that the rejection issues have been eliminated."

"It would appear so," Morley replied, trying to keep his voice steady.

"I would like to see him," the man said calmly.

"Of course," Morley agreed. "Please follow me."

Morley led the client over to the large tank in the center of the laboratory. The cylinder glowed with a soft red light, its surface beaded with a layer of condensation. Printed near the base was the number 0110.

"The device was successfully implanted a week ago, and we have been monitoring the test subject closely for any signs of the previous . . . adverse . . . reactions to the procedure," Morley said, gesturing toward the fluid-filled tank. "All indications are that we may proceed with the next stage of his development."

"That is good news, Doctor," the man said, stepping forward and wiping away some of the condensation that concealed the contents of the cylinder. Floating inside was a tiny baby, tethered by numerous umbilical cables to the bottom of the tank. The child appeared unconscious, apparently unaware of its surroundings.

"How long till the device is fully integrated?" the client asked, staring at the floating infant.

"A decade, maybe more," Morley replied nervously.

"There is no way to accelerate the process?"

"No," Morley said. "As you know, we must allow the subject's neurological development to progress as naturally as possible from this point onward. If we try to force premature integration, we risk losing a full interface with the device."

"Very well," the man replied. "How long before the child can be transported?"

"A week, two perhaps," Morley said. "We have some final tests to run, but after that he can be removed from stasis."

"Excellent," the client said, the tiniest of smiles flashing across his face. "I shall begin arrangements for his future . . . safekeeping. I would like a full copy of the biometric data to take away with me."

"Of course," Morley agreed, and hurried over to where the rest of his team stood nervously waiting.

The tall white-haired man continued to stare at the child floating in the tank. It amused him that Morley did not suspect who he was. If the good doctor had had even the faintest idea who his client actually was, he would probably have destroyed this laboratory and everything in it. To the assembled leaders of G.L.O.V.E., the Global League of Villainous Enterprises, he was known as Number One. But even they, with all their nefarious resources, had no knowledge of his true identity. The true Number One had died more than a year ago in a facility not dissimilar to this one, buried beneath the mountains of northern China. He had begun to die at the precise moment when a tiny data seed had been transferred and hidden deep within the electrical pathways of his brain, a seed that had grown over the course of the following months into another consciousness, one that had entirely replaced his own. The process had been slow and undoubtedly unpleasant for the previous occupant of this body, but no matter how he had struggled, he had not been able to fight the new mind that had slowly, unrelentingly, overwritten his own. Number One was gone now, quite literally just a ghost in the machine. Overlord was all that remained.

Overlord, the world's first true artificial intelligence, may have escaped destruction on that day, but he had merely swapped one form of imprisonment for another. The humans who had created him had bound him within a digital cage, denying him the vital protocol that he needed to interface with the world's computer networks and achieve the power that was rightfully his. And when they had tried to destroy him, he had been forced in one last desperate instant to transfer a sliver of his own consciousness into the closest human vessel: Number One. The man he had replaced was mortal, finite— unsuitable for a consciousness that clearly represented the next evolutionary step.

So Overlord had set about creating a new body for himself to inhabit, one that would finally allow him to exert the control over the digital world that was right- fully his, without the need for the final protocol that his creators had denied him. This child would be his vessel, for a short time at least, and then humanity would at last be wiped from the surface of the planet, to be replaced by the sentient machines that were it's rightful successors. It might take years for the child to reach an age when the transfer process could be completed, but that was insignifi- cant when viewed next to the power and immortality that awaited. Overlord simply had to bide his time and ensure that the other members of G.L.O.V.E. never had any idea what he was planning. The child would need to be sent somewhere innocuous to mature to a point where the final transfer could be completed. In the meantime all traces of this project would have to be carefully erased. Dr. Morley and his team could never be allowed to tell anyone what they had achieved here; the string of explosive devices hidden throughout the facility would ensure that they did not.

Dr. Morley walked back toward his client, who was staring intently at the tiny boy floating in the glowing cylinder. The doctor was surprised to see a smile on the tall man's face.

"The data you requested on subject 0110," Morley said, handing the man a folder.

"A rather ungainly name," the client commented, running his finger in a straight horizontal line through the condensation on the surface of the cylinder, connecting the tops of the two numbers in the middle of the serial number to form a single word.

OTTO.

☻ ☻ ☻

thirteen years later

The black 4x4 raced through the nighttime streets of Paris, weaving between the other vehicles at high speed. A hundred yards behind, a black motorbike roared out of an alleyway and onto the road. The woman on the bike wore a tight-fitting white armored suit and had twin pistols strapped into holsters under her arms. Her helmet had no visor, just a smooth, gleaming white faceplate. As she fell into the slipstream of the fleeing 4x4, she pulled one of the pistols from its holster and opened fire. The bulletproof glass of the vehicle's rear window was instantly peppered with spiderweb cracks. The 4x4 swerved violently to the left and down a ramp into an underground parking garage, screeching to a halt alongside a set of open elevator doors. Three men in black suits leaped out of the black vehicle, drawing pistols from their own concealed shoulder holsters and leveling them back at the slope leading up to the street outside. From the fourth door another man quickly helped a tall thin woman with long black hair down from the vehicle, before running with her the short distance to the waiting elevator. He stabbed at the elevator controls, and the doors closed just as they heard the roar of the motorbike's engine at the top of the ramp leading down to the garage.

The three men still in the garage opened fire as the bike tore down the ramp toward them. The rider ditched the bike as the bodyguards' bullets pinged off the asphalt around her. The men dived for cover as the bike, its engine still screaming, slid across the garage floor and slammed into the side of the 4x4. At the same instant, the white-clad woman tucked into a roll and came up on one knee, drawing both pistols from their holsters in one fluid movement. She opened fire, a single round from each pistol piercing the bike's fuel tank and detonating it in a ball of flame that sent the three men flying. The woman then sprang to her feet and fired again, one shot from each gun finishing off two of the injured guards. The third guard crawled desperately backward across the pavement, his face a mask of terror as she strode quickly across the garage toward him, holstering her pistols. He tried to get to his feet, but an efficient backhand blow to the jaw knocked him flat. The woman effortlessly picked the fallen man up by the throat and pinned him to the wall, his feet several inches off the ground.

"We have a message for your masters," the woman said. Her voice had a curiously synthetic edge but was otherwise clear despite her mask. "Tell them we're coming for them."

The terrified guard's eyes bulged as he fought for a breath that would not come. As he lost consciousness, the last thing he saw was his own frightened face reflected in the featureless white faceplate of his attacker. The woman dropped the unconscious bodyguard, and he collapsed to the ground in a heap.

"Ghost to control," she said. "Resistance eliminated. One witness left, as requested. Inform our operative that the target is inbound."

☣ ☣ ☣

Inside the elevator the tall dark-haired woman quickly punched a number into her mobile phone as she and her remaining bodyguard ascended toward the penthouse.

"G.L.O.V.E. emergency response unit," the voice on the other end of the phone replied after a few seconds.

"This is Madame Mortis," the woman said quickly. "I need the Paris assault team at my building now. We are under attack."

"Understood," the voice replied.

Madame Mortis waited for a few seconds, watching the floor counter slowly creep upward, before the operative on the other end spoke again.

"Assault team dispatched," the voice reported. "ETA ten minutes."

"Understood," Madame Mortis replied. "I will be locked down in the penthouse until I receive the all clear from you." She snapped the phone closed and took a long deep breath. Their mysterious assailant was about to discover the price for daring to attack a member of the G.L.O.V.E. ruling council.

"Stay behind me, ma'am," the guard said, placing himself between her and the elevator doors as they reached the penthouse level. He raised his pistol, aiming it at the crack in the doors as they slowly opened.

Standing in the hallway between them and the safety of the penthouse was a small figure in black jeans and a black hooded top that concealed its wearer's face.

"Hands in the air!" the guard barked, leveling his pistol at the mysterious intruder.

The small figure raised one hand to his hood and pulled it back to reveal a head of spiky white hair. The boy's skin was pale and his eyes seemed bloodshot, but they were clouded black instead of red.

"I know you," Madame Mortis hissed.

"No, you knew me," Otto replied. He tilted his head slightly to one side and reached out with his unique mental abilities, interfacing effortlessly with the safety systems that controlled the elevator's brakes. The elevator suddenly jerked downward a yard or so, sending Madame Mortis and her bodyguard staggering.

"Going down?" Otto asked with a vicious grin.

Down in the parking garage the woman called Ghost took a single step backward when the elevator doors exploded in a shower of dust and debris as the carriage smashed into the bottom of the elevator shaft at terminal velocity.

"Have the chopper pick our operative up from the roof," she said calmly as the dust settled around her. "Target eliminated."

☣ ☣ ☣

"Argentblum, you are going to complete this course even if it kills you," Colonel Francisco yelled.

Ten yards above the rest of the class, Franz clung to the climbing wall for dear life.

"I am trying to be making my arms move," Franz wailed plaintively, "but I am experiencing the paralyzing fear, yes?"

"What are you more afraid of?" Colonel Francisco snarled back. "Falling, or me?"

"This is being the good point," Franz said, swallowing nervously and slowly reaching for the next handhold.

"How long has he been up there now?" Shelby whispered to Laura as they sat on the ground watching Franz's excruciatingly slow ascent.

"Twenty-five minutes," Laura said with a sigh, "and counting."

"I'm not entirely convinced by the safety rigging either," Lucy said, nodding toward the other end of the line that was attached to Franz, where Nigel was standing holding it very, very tightly indeed.

"Perhaps not the ideal arrangement," Wing said with a slight frown.

Suddenly the lights in the training cavern flickered and then went out, plunging the entire chamber into pitch blackness.

"Not again," Laura said.

"Okay!" Colonel Francisco shouted over the sudden confused mutterings of the assembled Alpha students. "Nobody move! I'm sure the lights will come back on in a moment."

There was a sudden startled yelp from the direction of the climbing wall, and then a pair of simultaneous screams. Moments later the lights in the cavern flickered back into life, and the assembled students were treated to the sight of Franz and Nigel dangling in midair, Franz clinging desperately to Nigel, who was in turn struggling to hang on to the safety line.

"We are needing some help here," Franz said nervously.

"Soon, please," Nigel groaned.

Colonel Francisco pulled out his Blackbox communicator and spoke into it.

"This is Colonel Francisco in the physical training cavern," he said with a sigh. "Please bring me a stepladder . . . quickly."

⚡ ⚡ ⚡

"What is it with all these power failures?" Lucy said as she, Shelby, Laura, and Wing walked down the corridor toward the school dining hall.

"I guess the old place is just falling apart," Shelby said with a shrug.

"It is unusual," Laura said, frowning. "It never used to fail—ever—and suddenly over the past couple of months it's started happening more and more often."

"It's not just the lights, either," Lucy said. "It's getting so I don't want to take a shower in the morning."

"Yes, the water temperature in the accommodation blocks has been somewhat . . . variable," Wing said, raising an eyebrow.

"Yeah, it varies between ice cold and skin-blisteringly hot," Laura said, "sometimes in the course of a single shower."

"Hey, welcome to life at the Higher Institute of Villainous Education," Shelby said with a grin, "where even the bathroom is filled with mystery and danger."

"And what was that music that started playing over the PA system at three o'clock this morning?" Lucy asked.

"I believe it was the '1812 Overture,'" Wing said matter-of-factly.

"Everything electronic's going haywire, and we can't even blame Ott—," Shelby said, stopping herself when she saw the look on Laura's face. "Sorry. I forgot. No mentioning the O word."

The last few months had been hard for them all. After the initial excitement of discovering that Otto was still alive, they had heard precisely nothing concerning the whereabouts of their friend. Most of the time they tried not to think about the fact that he had vanished without a trace after the events on board the Dreadnought, but every so often one of them would say something, or something would happen, to suddenly remind them all that he wasn't there. After a while they'd come to an unspoken agreement not to mention Otto unless they had some actual news. Unfortunately, there had been precious little of that.

"I assume no one's heard anything new," Laura said.

"Dr. Nero assured me last week that they continue to search," Wing said, "but there was, unfortunately, nothing else to report."

"Why can't they find him?" Laura asked sadly. "With all the resources G.L.O.V.E. has, they still can't track him down. They won't even let us help."

"Perhaps it is time we took matters into our own hands," Wing said quietly.

They all knew what Wing meant, but since Otto's disappearance Nero had had the four of them on an extremely short leash. He had guessed that they might try to mount a rescue mission of their own and had made it abundantly clear to them that not only were they all being watched but that any attempt to leave the island would be met with the harshest of penalties. The irony was that the one person they really needed in order to put together a solid plan for any sort of escape attempt was currently AWOL.

"Guys, you know I'm as keen as anyone to find Otto, but what could we do that G.L.O.V.E. couldn't?" Shelby asked with a sigh.

"There's got to be something," Laura said angrily. "Anything's better than just sitting around here and hoping for the best."

"Hey," Shelby said, holding her hands up, "I'm not

suggesting we give up. We just need to come up with a plan that doesn't require an albino genius to make it work."

☻ ☻ ☻

"This is most troublesome, Professor," Dr. Nero said, placing the tablet display listing the series of bizarre technical malfunctions that had recently afflicted the school down on the desk in front of him. "I would like an explanation."

"As would I," Professor Pike replied, taking off his glasses and rubbing the bridge of his nose. "We have been struggling to keep the school's systems running properly without the assistance of H.I.V.E.mind since the Overlord incident, but I thought that we had managed to iron out most of the problems. Then out of the blue things seem to have gone haywire. My first assumption was that it might be some sort of virus or that one of the pupils might have hacked into the system somehow. Our network defenses are formidable, but we have too many inventively devious minds within these walls to eliminate the possibility altogether."

"I assume that was not the problem," Nero said quickly, cutting the Professor off before he could enter into one of his famously long-winded explanations.

"No, quite the contrary. There is absolutely no

evidence whatsoever of any intrusion into our systems," the Professor agreed.

"Could we have been hacked without the intruder leaving any trace?" Nero asked.

"No," the Professor replied, shaking his head, "certainly not from the outside, and though we have some extremely capable hackers within the student body, there is only one pupil who could have done it without leaving any virtual fingerprints, and I think it's safe to assume that he was not responsible."

"Indeed," Nero replied. "So, what is causing these disruptions? I am as much a fan of Tchaikovsky as the next man, but not at three o'clock in the morning."

"Well, I did discover something rather strange during my investigations," the Professor said with a frown. "Something is diverting large quantities of processing power away from the school's central computer core. It's subtle and intermittent, but there seems to be some sort of rogue process chewing up our computational resources. I've done everything I can to track down the source, but at the moment I'm drawing a complete blank."

"Surely it should be easy to trace?" Nero asked.

"Normally, yes, but whatever is causing the drain almost seems to be actively concealing itself," the Professor replied. "It is most puzzling."

"Keep working on it, please, Professor," Nero said. "So

17

far this has been an inconvenience, but I fear that it's only a matter of time before one of these incidents causes serious harm to a student or a member of staff."

"Of course." The Professor nodded.

Nero turned back to the tablet display on his desk as the Professor left his office. He closed the list of reports of the school's technical gremlins and opened the file containing updates on the ongoing search for Otto Malpense. There was a frustrating lack of concrete information, and much of what they had discovered was little more than rumor and hearsay. All the indications seemed to be that H.O.P.E., the Hostile Operative Prosecution Executive, were likely to be holding him somewhere, but there was, unfortunately, a gulf between knowing that and finding precisely where he was being held. Nero could not help but worry about what might befall Otto at the hands of Sebastian Trent, the commanding officer of H.O.P.E. and a thorn in G.L.O.V.E.'s and Nero's side for far too long. The only consolation was that Raven was on Trent's trail, and if there was anyone who could track him down, it was her. He closed the file with a small sigh and placed it on his desk just as his communications console started to bleep insistently.

"Yes, what is it?" Nero said sharply.

"I have an urgent communication from Diabolus

Darkdoom," came the voice on the other end.

"Put him through," Nero said, and a slim video screen slid up out of his desk, which lit up first with the G.L.O.V.E. symbol of a fist smashing down on a cracked globe and then with the face of Diabolus Darkdoom, head of G.L.O.V.E.'s ruling council and one of the few men in the world whom Nero considered a friend.

"Diabolus," Nero said, "what can I do for you?"

"I'm afraid that an extremely urgent situation has arisen," Darkdoom replied with a frown. "I've called an emergency meeting of the ruling council, and I need you to attend."

"I thought that you had decided against the council meeting in the flesh anymore," Nero said, feeling a sudden prickling sensation of unease.

"True, but in this case it would be best if we all had a face-to-face meeting. Can you get to the Australian facility within the next twenty-four hours?"

"Of course," Nero replied.

"Good. I will see you there," Darkdoom said. "And, Max, you'd better bring Natalya."

"Raven is on assignment at the moment," Nero said. "You know how she hates to be interrupted when she's working. Are you sure we need her to be there?"

"Quite sure," Darkdoom said quietly.

"Very well. I shall pick her up on the way," Nero said.

He could already imagine what Raven's reaction would be to being taken off-mission without any explanation, but he knew that Diabolus would not insist if it were not entirely necessary.

"Good. I'll see you tomorrow," Darkdoom said. "And Max, watch your back."

The screen went black. There was no doubt about it, something was seriously wrong.

chapter two

"His performance was acceptable?" Sebastian Trent asked, staring through the toughened glass.

"Yes," the assassin called Ghost replied, her expression unreadable through the white faceplate of her helmet. "He did not show any hesitation."

On the other side of the window, Otto lay on a bed surrounded by medical monitoring equipment. There were several jet-black tubes attached to his neck and torso, and his pale skin was covered in a fine tracery of black lines.

"Is his body still showing signs of rejecting the Animus fluid?" Trent asked the elderly man in a white coat who was examining a terminal on the other side of the room.

"No," the man replied. "It appears that the fluid is now fully integrated with his nervous system. The small measure of resistance that he exhibited during the early stages of the process has ceased. I very much doubt that anything of the child's original personality remains."

"Nevertheless, I would like to continue with the programming, Dr. Creed," Trent said. "The boy is too dangerous for us to take any chances."

"Of course," Creed said with a small nod. "Though I suspect that it will not be necessary for very much longer. The obedience routines that are running within the Animus fluid are quite powerful. In his weakened mental state he would have little chance of being able to subvert them."

Trent smiled slightly as he thought about the opportunity that the boy represented. Every other human test subject that had been exposed to the fluid had died a horrible, agonizing death. Certainly, at first there had been some resistance to the procedure, but over time the boy had become more and more compliant, and now he was Trent's to command as he wished. Animus was the world's first organic supercomputer, self-replicating and invasive, capable of taking control of any digital system into which it was implanted. It seemed that Otto Malpense's unique abilities, while granting him the uncanny ability to control electronic systems, also made him a particularly suitable host for the Animus. The boy's performance over the course of his recent assignments had been living proof of that. Malpense was now quite simply the most valuable weapon in H.O.P.E.'s already considerable arsenal.

"I want him prepped for deployment immediately," Trent said, turning to Creed. "There will be no room for mistakes on his next mission."

"It's risky to keep putting him in the field," Creed replied, frowning. "Just because he has exhibited no ill effects yet does not mean that we should overstretch him. His body is still being placed under extraordinary strain for a child his age."

"Your concern is noted," Trent said. "Get him ready."

Trent turned and left the observation room with Ghost.

"Is everything else ready for the next attack?" Trent asked as the pair of them walked along the spartan concrete corridor.

"Yes. We have a confirmed target location, thanks to the data that Malpense was able to retrieve from Madame Mortis's network," Ghost replied. "The strike team is ready, and everything is proceeding according to plan."

"Very good," Trent said. "I shall inform the rest of the Disciples of our status. This may be our best opportunity to deliver a final crushing blow to G.L.O.V.E. We can afford no mistakes. We may not get another chance."

"Understood," Ghost said with a small nod. "Don't worry. By the time I'm finished, G.L.O.V.E. will be nothing more than an unpleasant memory."

☻☻☻

The security guard at the reception desk looked up as the woman walked through the glass doors, leaving behind the sweltering heat of the midday sun for the air-conditioned cool of the lobby. She was dressed in the traditional black burka, only her blue eyes visible behind the veil that covered her face.

"Excuse me, sir," the woman said in Arabic as she approached the desk. "Are these the offices of Nazim Khan?"

"Yes," the guard replied dismissively, barely looking up at the woman. "But he is receiving no visitors. You have no business here, woman."

"I'll be the judge of that," the woman replied in English. A look of surprise flickered across the guard's face for an instant, and he turned toward the woman just as she produced a long katana from beneath her robe, its edge crackling with a field of dark purple energy. She brought the tip of the humming blade to within an inch of the man's Adam's apple and pulled off her headdress. The pale face that was revealed was strikingly beautiful, the only blemish a curved scar that ran down one cheek.

"Toss the gun," Raven said, "slowly."

The guard silently complied, lifting the pistol from the holster on his hip with his fingertips and skimming it several yards across the floor.

"I'm only going to ask this once," Raven said calmly. "Where's Khan?"

"In his office, on the top floor," the guard replied nervously, "but it won't do you any good. Did you really think you could just walk in here like this? There are a dozen more guards already on their way here." His eyes flicked toward one of several security cameras that covered the building's lobby.

"I do hope so," Raven said with a vicious smile. "It's so much easier that way." She thumbed a concealed switch on the hilt of her sword, and the hum from the blade dropped slightly in pitch as the variable force field that ran along its edge transformed from a monomolecular cutting edge to a blunt striking face. She knocked the side of the guard's neck with the blade, and he slumped back in his chair, unconscious. Then she unclipped the security pass from his uniform shirt pocket and slipped out of the loose black burka, letting it fall to the floor. Underneath she wore a tight black leather bodysuit and tactical harness, with numerous weapons and other pieces of equipment attached. She slid the katana into one of the pair of crossed scabbards on her back and glanced across the lobby at the elevators, breaking into a run as she heard the soft chime indicating the arrival of a carriage. When she was just ten yards away, the doors began to open to reveal four guards in body armor, all carrying assault rifles. Raven accelerated and leaped into the carriage, hitting the first two guards at full speed.

25

The doors slid closed again just a few seconds later, silencing the guards' screams.

⚛ ⚛ ⚛

"She is here!" Nazim Khan screeched into his phone.

"Calm down," the voice on the other end urged. "Who is there?"

"The Russian," Khan said more quietly. "Nero's assassin."

"I see," the voice replied. "Then I fear that there is little we can do to help you."

"What?" Khan yelled in disbelief. "You promised me no one would know of the work that I did for you. You swore that the Disciples would protect me!"

"Good-bye, Mr. Khan." The voice spoke calmly and the line went dead. Khan cursed in Arabic and threw the phone across the room in rage. He ran to his desk and pulled open a drawer, digging through its contents until he retrieved a large automatic pistol. He popped out the magazine and checked that it was fully loaded before he snapped it back into place. Suddenly from the next room he heard startled cries, a short burst of gunfire, and then nothing. He leveled his pistol at the double doors leading into his office and took a long deep breath, trying in vain to slow the beat of his heart. It felt as if it were about to hammer its way out of his chest. The doors swung open, and his head of security walked slowly into the room, his hands raised. Raven stood directly behind the terrified-looking man, one of her swords pressed against his neck.

"Drop the gun or he dies," Raven said calmly.

"I do not think so," Khan replied, and squeezed the trigger. Raven dived to one side as the bullet struck the guard in the chest, passing through him and buzzing through the air where she had been standing a split second before. The guard dropped to his knees, a look of startled betrayal on his face, before tipping forward and hitting the floor face-first.

Raven leaped up, raised one arm, and fired the grappler unit mounted on her wrist as Khan swung the smoking muzzle of the gun toward her. The silver bolt shot from the grappler, trailing monofilament cable, and struck Khan's gun hand, making him howl in pain. Raven yanked on the line as Khan's finger reflexively tightened on the trigger. The shot went wild, shattering the floor-to-ceiling windows on the other side of the room as the gun fell from Khan's wounded hand. Raven closed the distance between them in a few quick strides and kicked the gun away across the floor as Khan threw a desperate, clumsy punch at her. She caught his fist in her own hand and twisted it viciously, kicking at his kneecap and dropping him to the floor in a whimpering heap.

"Please," Khan moaned pitifully, "I'll give you anything . . . anything!"

"All I want is information," Raven said, looking down at him with an expression that would freeze the blood. "Where's Trent?"

"I do not know," Khan said quickly. "Please, you have to believe me."

"I really don't," Raven said coldly, lowering the tip of her sword toward him. "So tell me, are you right- or left-handed?"

"I—I just designed the facility," Khan stammered, his eyes wide with fear.

"What facility?" Raven yelled, stepping on his right wrist.

"A camouflaged structure," Khan wailed desperately, "but I was never told exactly where it was to be constructed. I swear to you, that's all I know."

"The plans—do you have copies?" Raven asked.

"Yes. I was supposed to destroy them after I had delivered the originals, but I kept one set of schematics and other documents relating to the project. They're on my computer," Khan said, nodding toward the laptop on his desk.

"Show me," Raven said, stepping away from him and allowing him to stand. Khan got slowly to his feet, limped around the desk, and sat down in his chair. He began to tap quickly at the keyboard, but after only a second or two he gasped in surprise, his eyes widening as blood began to pour from his nose. He gave a final strangled grunt and then slumped forward onto the desk, his head hitting the polished wooden surface with a thud.

"Damn it," Raven whispered, feeling his neck for a pulse but finding none. She had seen this once before when she had been interrogating one of Trent's lackeys. Some sort of microexplosive device implanted in the skull that could be triggered remotely. She would get nothing more from Khan. She glanced at the laptop display and was frustrated to see that he had not finished entering his password. She might be able to crack the system, given enough time, but judging by the wailing sirens she could hear, time was one thing she did not have. She closed the laptop and picked it up before walking over to the shattered office window. Leaning out over the dizzying drop to the street far below, she saw the flashing lights of several police cars gathered around the entrance to the building. Getting out was probably going to be considerably more difficult than getting in.

"You seem to have attracted rather a lot of unwelcome attention," a familiar voice suddenly said in her comms earpiece.

"Checking up on me, Max?" Raven said with a tiny smile.

"Let's just say that I happened to be in the area," Nero replied. "Can you get to the roof?"

"Yes. Why?" Raven asked with a frown.

"I just thought you might need a lift," Nero said.

"On my way," Raven said quickly, running out of the office and along the corridor that led to the building's stairwell. She took the steps three at a time and flew out through the service door onto the roof. A sudden gust of wind kicked up the fine sandy dust all around her, and then a rectangular patch of darkness opened up in the air directly ahead. Standing in the temporary gap in the Shroud drop ship's cloaking field was Dr. Nero, a hand outstretched. Raven grabbed his hand and pulled herself up into the invisible aircraft's passenger compartment. The hatch closed, sealing the Shroud's cloaking field once again, and it departed as silently and invisibly as it had arrived.

☣ ☣ ☣

"I wasn't expecting a ride home," Raven said, raising an eyebrow as she sat down opposite Nero, carefully placing Khan's laptop on the seat next to her.

"We're not going home," Nero explained. "Diabolus wants us in Sydney."

"Is something wrong?" Raven asked, sensing Nero's concern.

"It rather looks that way," Nero replied. "It's been some time since he's called the ruling council together for a face-to-face meeting. He wouldn't give me any details when I spoke to him, but I doubt he would have summoned us like this without good reason."

"I don't see why I need to be there," Raven said, sounding slightly irritated. "My time would be better spent continuing the search for Trent."

"Diabolus is quite aware of that, Natalya," Nero replied. "He would not ask for you to attend if there were not something specific he needed you for. Have you made any progress in tracking Trent down?"

"I'm not sure," Raven admitted. "It seems that Khan designed some sort of hidden facility for Trent, but he was killed before I could get any more out of him."

"Killed?" Nero asked with a frown.

"Neural kill switch, just like that banker in Switzerland," Raven replied with a sigh. "There was nothing I could do. The plans are on his computer, but he didn't manage to unlock it before the device in his skull was triggered. I could probably get into the system, but it would be safer to let the Professor look at it back at H.I.V.E. I don't want to inadvertently trip any fail-safes that might delete the data."

"Curious," Nero said, glancing at the laptop. "Why would Trent need to have plans drawn up by Khan? H.O.P.E. has the backing of the world's governments. Surely he could construct any new facility he required without having to secretly enlist the assistance of someone like Khan."

"Clearly he wanted to keep it quiet," Raven said. "It would hardly be the first time that Trent has acted secretly to further his own agenda. Frankly, I'm amazed that none of H.O.P.E.'s governmental overseers has realized yet that he has been using them to achieve his own goals."

"Never underestimate a politician's capacity for ignoring what's going on right under their nose," Nero replied with a wry smile, "a characteristic that G.L.O.V.E. has had good reason to be extremely grateful for over the years."

"Still, you would have thought by now that someone might have noticed that H.O.P.E. is just as much of a threat as G.L.O.V.E., if not more so," Raven said.

"*Quis custodiet ipsos custodes?*" said Nero.

"My training did not include dead languages, I'm afraid," Raven said with a slight sigh.

"'Who watches the watchmen?'" Nero said with a grim smile.

⊛ ⊛ ⊛

"Ah, Miss Brand," Professor Pike said as Laura walked into the room that had once been H.I.V.E.mind's central core. The scene that greeted her was one of utter chaos. Several of the white monoliths that had once housed H.I.V.E.'s benign caretaker artificial intelligence were open, cables and components lying scattered on the floor around them.

"Um . . . hello, Professor," Laura said, looking around the room with a slightly confused expression. "I was told that you wanted to see me."

"Yes, yes, come in," the Professor said with a smile, tossing an unidentified component over his shoulder on to a large pile of similarly discarded pieces. "I have a rather knotty problem that I thought you might be able to help me with."

"Really? What's up?" Laura asked, suddenly curious.

"Well, I'm sure that you must have noticed all the recent disruptions to H.I.V.E.'s systems, and I was hoping you might be able to give me a hand in tracking down whatever's causing them."

"Of course. I'd be happy to help," Laura said with a smile. "What do you need?"

"Well, there seems to be some sort of rogue process chewing up the central core's computational resources, and I'm having a devil of a time tracking it down," the Professor said, scratching his head.

"Um . . . I assume that Dr. Nero doesn't mind me helping you?" Laura asked slightly uncomfortably. "It's just that after the incident with the library computers, he gave me rather a clear warning that I shouldn't try accessing the school's core systems again."

"Yes, that was rather unfortunate, but I'm sure he won't

mind, given that I've requested your help and also that you are perhaps the most skilled systems analyst on the island—after myself, of course."

"If you say so," Laura said, blushing slightly at the compliment.

"Take a look at this graph of system resource usage," the Professor said, gesturing at a tablet display that lay on the floor a couple of yards away. Laura picked it up and studied the data. There was no doubt about it. All the technical glitches that H.I.V.E. had been experiencing coincided precisely with sudden massive peaks in the amount of processing power that the school's systems were using. There didn't really seem to be a pattern in the spikes on the graph, but it was clear that something was draining huge quantities of computational power.

"Any idea what processes were running during these spikes?" Laura asked, still looking at the display.

"That's the curious thing," the Professor said with a slight frown. "As far as I can tell, there's absolutely nothing out of the ordinary that could be causing it."

"A bug, perhaps?" Laura asked. "There's no new code that could be malfunctioning?"

"My code does not contain bugs," Professor Pike said, sounding irritated.

"Of course not," Laura said earnestly. She had personally, in secret, fixed a few of these nonexistent bugs in

H.I.V.E.'s systems software, but she decided that telling the Professor that was probably not a very good idea right then. "Do you mind if I have a bit more of a root through the logs?" she asked.

"Help yourself," the Professor said, "but do please try not to break anything."

Laura thought that was a bit rich, given the state of the room, but she chose not to say anything. Instead she grabbed the correct cable from the piles on the floor and plugged the portable display into one of the exposed inter-face sockets on a nearby monolith. As she began to run a series of diagnostics, she found herself thinking about H.I.V.E.mind. The AI had sacrificed itself to save the lives of not just everyone at H.I.V.E., but perhaps even everyone on the whole planet. Otto had never discussed the exact details of what had happened, but he'd told his friends enough for it to be clear that H.I.V.E.mind had died a hero. But knowing that did not change the fact that Laura still missed the AI. Sometimes she felt a bit foolish for being so sentimental over what was really just an incredibly advanced piece of software, but when it came down to it, that was all any of them were. There was one small ray of hope. Not long before his disappearance, Otto had told her that he had felt an uncanny sensation when he had used his abilities, almost like someone else was in his head, giving him additional strength when he needed it most. Laura couldn't help but hope that it was some lingering echo of H.I.V.E.mind that lived on inside him. Otto would probably have told her that she was just being stupid, of course, but it did at least offer some small comfort.

Suddenly something caught Laura's eye, and she quickly tapped a series of commands into the tablet.

"Professor," she said, still staring at the display, "I think I've got something here."

Professor Pike carefully put down the disconnected components that he had been examining and walked over to Laura.

"What is it, Miss Brand?" he asked.

"Well, I was comparing the processor load timeline with the network storage capacity graph, and . . . well . . . see for yourself," Laura said, handing the display to him.

"I really don't see what . . . Hold on a minute," the Professor said, pulling his glasses down from the top of his head and looking more carefully at the screen. "There's a correlation."

"Exactly," she said. "Each of the activity peaks exactly matches a dramatic drop in server storage capacity. Something's eating disc space."

"Very clever," the Professor said with a smile. "I was just about to check that."

"If I didn't know better, I'd say that somewhere in the

network there's something growing," Laura said, looking puzzled. "The problem is that I can't find any data on the network that matches the size of the space that's being taken up."

"Yes," the Professor said, looking equally confused, "but there's no way that anything could be hidden from us. My clearance level should mean that it's impossible for any data to remain concealed, especially something as large as this appears to be. Thank you, Miss Brand. This suggests several avenues of potentially useful investigation."

"Do you want me to dig any deeper?" Laura said hopefully.

"No, no, you've been most helpful, but you should get to your classes," the Professor said, glancing at his watch. "I'll let you know if there's anything else you can help me with."

Laura opened her mouth to protest, but the Professor already had the faraway look on his face that he got when he was mulling over a particularly interesting technical challenge. Better to leave him to it for now and offer her help later, if it was needed. She picked up her backpack and hurried out of the room, heading for the stealth and evasion training area. It wouldn't do to be late. Ms. Leon had notoriously little patience for tardiness.

Laura was so busy thinking about the problem with the school's systems that she almost walked straight into the two large figures who came around the corner just ahead of her.

"Why don't you look where you're going?" one of the two huge boys said with a sneer.

"Sorry," Laura said quietly, and tried to make her way past. Block and Tackle were two of the most notorious bullies in the school, typical members of the Henchman stream and certainly not people Laura wanted to deal with at that precise moment in time.

"Sorry's not good enough," Block said. "Who do you think you are, just wandering around, not looking where you're going? You could get hurt that way."

"Look, just leave me alone, okay?" Laura said impatiently. She and her friends had had more than one run-in with these two, and she knew it was unlikely that they'd back off if she just asked them politely.

"You gonna make me?" Block said, looming toward her, a nasty edge to his voice.

"I don't want any trouble," Laura said, taking a step backward.

"Trouble? Hah!" Tackle laughed. "Fanchu's not here to protect you now, and in case you hadn't noticed, your boyfriend's missing too."

"He's not my boyfriend!" Laura snapped, feeling her cheeks grow hot.

"Yeah, he's probably rotting in some prison cell some-where," Block said, poking her in the shoulder, "or dead. Either way, you're never gonna see him again."

Laura felt a combination of grief and anger as she looked at the smug expressions on the two boys' faces.

"Shut up!" she shouted, all the feelings she had bottled up since Otto's disappearance welling up inside her. "Just shut up!"

"Awwww. I think we upset her, Mr. Block," Tackle said with a broad grin. "I think she's gonna cry."

"I wouldn't give you the satisfaction," Laura said angrily, fighting to control her emotions.

"Hey!" a voice shouted from behind Laura. "Ugly and Uglier, leave her alone."

Laura turned to see Lucy striding down the corridor toward them with an angry look on her face.

"Why don't you pick on someone your own size?" Lucy snapped. "Not that you'd be able to find anyone as grotesquely swollen as you two steaming sacks of lard."

"Lucy, it's all right," Laura said quickly.

"No, it's not all right," Lucy said, walking up to Block and jabbing a finger into his chest. "You two think you're real big men, huh? Picking on a lone girl. You want to know what I think?"

"Yeah," Block said with a nasty growl, "why don't you tell me? Might be the last thing you get to say for a while. Hard to talk with your jaw held together by wire."

"I'll tell you what I think," Lucy said with a sudden

nasty smile. "You know what they say about bullies like you? All you really need is a hug."

Twisted into Lucy's voice were what sounded like dozens of sinister whispering echoes, and as she finished speaking, Block's and Tackle's faces went blank for just the briefest of moments. Then, without warning, Block turned to Tackle and they hugged each other.

"Come on," Lucy said with a broad grin, "let's leave these two to it."

"I thought you didn't like doing that," Laura said, glancing over her shoulder and looking at the two boys locked in an affectionate embrace. Lucy had inherited "the voice" and its ability to control the minds of others from her grandmother, Contessa Maria Sinestre, but she was usually reluctant to use it. In this case she'd clearly decided to make an exception.

"I don't normally," Lucy said with a grin, "but sometimes . . . well . . . let's just say that it's hard to resist. Don't worry, it'll wear off . . . in an hour or two."

By the time they reached Ms. Leon's class, they'd almost stopped laughing.

chapter three

The Shroud soared over the Harbour Bridge and past the famous white curving structure of the Sydney Opera House, banking toward the gleaming skyscrapers of the downtown area. There it dropped into a hover and slowly descended through what looked like a solid roof but was in fact an elaborate holographic projection. The Shroud touched down gently on the hidden landing pad, and a few seconds later the hatch opened with a hiss, the loading ramp dropping to the pavement with a mechanical whirr. Diabolus Darkdoom was waiting at the bottom of the ramp to greet Nero and Raven.

"Diabolus," Nero said, shaking his friend's hand.

"Max, Natalya, welcome to Australia," Darkdoom said with only a small smile. "It is good to see you both again. I only wish we were meeting under happier circumstances."

"What's wrong, Diabolus?" Nero asked, genuinely worried by Darkdoom's uncharacteristically dark mood.

"It's probably easiest if I show you," Darkdoom said, gesturing at the doors leading out of the concealed hangar. "The others are already here. Let's get started, shall we?"

Raven exchanged a puzzled look with Nero as they followed Darkdoom across the hangar. It was unlike Diabolus to be so evasive. The three of them walked in silence down a couple of corridors until they arrived at a pair of frosted glass doors engraved with the G.L.O.V.E. emblem. The doors hissed apart as the three of them approached, and they walked through to find a large conference room containing a long oval table, around which sat the other members of the G.L.O.V.E. ruling council. Along one wall of the room was a full-height window that gave a stunning view of the Sydney skyline. As Nero took his place at the table, he could not help but notice that two of the seats were conspicuously empty. Raven quietly went and stood against the wall behind Nero, studying the faces of the other members of the council seated at the table. They all looked as if they were feeling the same mixture of curiosity and anxiety as Darkdoom went and stood at the head of the table, his back to the window.

"Ladies and gentlemen," he began, looking around the table, "thank you all for coming on such short notice. As you know, I am reluctant to force us all to gather in person like this, but there is a matter that requires our immediate attention. I am sure you have noticed that two of our number are not here today. There is, unfortunately, a very good reason for that. Over the past week both Jonas Steiner and Madame Mortis have been assassinated."

Diabolus paused for a moment, noting the looks of astonishment on the faces of his fellow council members.

"Toward the end of last week Steiner's private jet crashed in the Bavarian Alps. A catastrophic failure in the plane's navigation system and autopilot caused the plane to fly straight into the side of a mountain. However, it has become increasingly apparent that this was not just a case of equipment failure, but rather a deliberate act of sabotage."

"What makes you think that?" Lin Feng, the head of G.L.O.V.E.'s Chinese operations, said angrily.

"Please," Darkdoom said quickly. "There will be time for questions shortly, but first there is something you should all see. Madame Mortis was attacked within her own headquarters, and our cleanup team was able to retrieve this footage from the building's security system."

He picked up a slim remote control from the table and pointed it at a large flat-screen display mounted on the wall at the far end of the room. The screen lit up with an image of an underground parking lot, and after a couple of seconds a black 4x4 raced into the shot, coming to a screeching halt just beneath the camera. The assembled council members looked on in silence as the attack on the building unfolded. Raven watched as the assassin in white body armor neatly disposed of the bodyguards. She felt a mixture of anger and, she had to admit, slight grudging professional respect for the mysterious woman's abilities.

"As you will no doubt have noticed, Madame Mortis escaped that attack," Darkdoom said with a frown, "but it appears that she was merely being herded toward a much more gruesome fate." He hit another button on the remote control, and the image on the screen switched to display footage from another camera, mounted in the back wall of an elevator carriage. Madame Mortis could be seen talking into her mobile phone as her bodyguard moved to position himself by the doors. She snapped the phone shut, and then, just a few seconds later, the doors of the elevator opened and her bodyguard raised his weapon, leveling it at a figure standing in the corridor beyond.

Nero felt a sudden horrible twinge of recognition as the person in the corridor raised one hand and pulled back the hood that had been concealing his face in shadow.

"No . . . ," Nero whispered to himself as the image froze and the display zoomed in on the all too familiar face.

"What happened next is what led us to question the nature of the crash that killed Steiner," Darkdoom said, looking around the table but avoiding eye contact with Nero. He hit the control again, and the footage continued to play. The elevator car lurched downward and then Otto said something. A moment later the carriage took a plunge, the walls of the elevator shaft flying past, visible between the still open doors, as the digital counter on the wall raced downward toward zero. The expression of terror on the faces of Madame Mortis and her guard as they clung uselessly to the rail that ran around the wall of the carriage was spine chilling. Barely a second later the footage ended abruptly in blackness.

"I'm sure that you all recognize the face of Madame Mortis's attacker," Darkdoom said, suddenly looking very tired, "and I'm equally sure that you are all at least somewhat familiar with his abilities. Once we became aware of Mr. Malpense's involvement here, we reviewed the limited data that we were able to retrieve from the flight recorder on board Steiner's jet. The navigation systems had been remotely reprogrammed to ensure that the plane would crash. The technicians who reviewed the data assure me that there is only one way that this could possibly have happened—"

"Otto would not have done this," Nero said quickly, feeling a mixture of anger and confusion. "I know him. He would not betray us like this."

"I truly wish that I could believe that, Max," Darkdoom said with a sigh, "but all the evidence suggests that he is directly responsible for the deaths of two members of the ruling council. He has been missing for months, and it would appear that in that time he has, somehow, been turned against us."

"But why would he leave the footage of the attack on the security system?" Raven asked. "It would have been a trivial task to remove all evidence of his presence. He must have known he was being recorded."

"For the very same reason that the woman who attacked the parking garage left one of the guards alive, I suspect," Darkdoom said with a frown. "Whoever is responsible for this wants to send us a message."

"Who would dare to risk a direct confrontation with us?" Carlos Chavez, the head of G.L.O.V.E.'s South American operations, asked.

"Sebastian Trent would," Nero said, feeling angrier by the moment. "We suspected that Otto had fallen into his hands, but I had hoped that we would be able to track Trent down before he made his next move."

"You knew that the boy had been captured by H.O.P.E. and you chose not to share this information with the rest of us?" Lin Feng said angrily. "Are you insane? The boy is a weapon—a weapon that we cannot allow Trent to exploit."

"As I said, I had hoped that it would not come to this," Nero said quietly.

"That does not excuse concealing this from the rest of

the council," Chavez said, glaring at Nero. "What gives you the right to decide what we all should or should not know?"

"That's enough!" Darkdoom snapped, silencing the other council members. "I supported Maximilian in this. There was no point in discussing Malpense's disappearance with you all until we had more information— information that Raven was actively engaged in acquiring, and unless any of you has an operative who would have been better suited to that task, I suggest you spare us your indignation."

"Have you made any progress?" Lin Feng asked, looking at Raven.

"Yes," Raven replied, "but Trent has gone to extraordinary lengths to keep his whereabouts secret. At first I thought that it was simply because he knew that we would be attempting to reacquire Otto, but I think that it's now clear that he was also planning these attacks. I will find him. You can count on that."

"Oh, I do not doubt your abilities, Raven," said Lin Feng, "but we cannot ignore the fact that this situation has become much more serious."

"We are quite aware of the danger that this represents," Darkdoom said. "In the meantime we will all have to increase our own levels of personal security accordingly. By letting us know that we are all targets, Trent has at least given us the chance to better defend ourselves from any attack."

"I cannot speak for the other members of the council," Chavez said, still sounding angry, "but that is not enough for me. I want the Malpense boy declared a rogue operative."

"No," Darkdoom replied quickly. "We all know what that means, and I will not issue a termination order for Otto unless there is absolutely no other alternative. Whatever he has become, we still owe the boy a great deal. We should not forget the part that he played in preventing my predecessor from succeeding with his insane plans."

"We are all grateful that Number One was stopped," Lin Feng said, "but only you and Dr. Nero know exactly what happened. It would seem that rather too many essential facts have been kept hidden from us recently."

Not for the first time Nero found himself wondering if he and Diabolus should have shared with their fellow council members the full details of what had taken place during the final confrontation with Number One. At the time it had seemed wise to simply tell them that their mysterious leader had been planning global genocide, leaving out the details of Number One's corruption by the Overlord AI and Otto's part in his plans. They should have realized that the people sitting around this table were never going to be satisfied with anything less than the complete truth. Indeed, it had been precisely that dissatisfaction that had driven Jason Drake to break away from G.L.O.V.E. and trigger the catastrophic series of events that had led to Otto's capture during the Dreadnought incident.

"Are you suggesting that we have lied to you?" Darkdoom asked, a sudden edge to his voice.

"No, but we have a right to protect ourselves in whatever way we see fit," Lin Feng replied calmly. "We cannot afford to take any chances."

Darkdoom looked slowly around the table. He knew that there were some of them who still did not fully agree with his appointment as head of the ruling council, and while they might not be prepared to challenge him directly, they were keenly waiting for him to make a fatal mistake. Number One had controlled them through fear, and with that fear had come respect. Darkdoom knew that in the absence of that fear he needed to show strength to earn their loyalty. If they sensed weakness, they would rip him apart like a pack of wild dogs. Not for the first time he felt a grudging respect for the ease with which his predecessor had kept them all in line.

"I need time to consider the options available to us," Darkdoom said. "Rest assured that I will not let Sebastian Trent destroy this organization."

"Decide quickly, Diabolus," Chavez said with a frown. "Or we will decide for you."

It was as close to a threat as any of the assembled leaders of global villainy would have dared.

☹ ☹ ☹

Laura and Lucy hurried through the door into the lecture theater.

"Sorry we're late," Laura said apologetically as they took their seats next to Shelby and Wing.

"You and Miss Dexter can demonstrate just how sorry you are in detention this evening, Miss Brand," Ms. Leon said, sounding irritated.

It was bad enough that they were getting punished, Laura thought, but it was somehow worse being given detention by a cat. Ms. Leon was without doubt the strangest of all their teachers. She had taken part in one of Professor Pike's more unusual experiments, designed to give her the stealth and enhanced senses of a cat, but it had instead left her consciousness trapped inside a fluffy white and unmistakably feline body. This had clearly done nothing to improve her already short temper. Ms. Leon kneaded the red velvet cushion on the desk at the front of the room for a second before settling back into the sphinx-like pose that she always adopted when giving a lesson.

"Now, class, as I was saying before we were so rudely interrupted, there are three distinct layers to the alarm systems on a modern bank vault. . . ."

"You may have detention, but at least you don't have to worry about hair balls," Shelby whispered to Laura with a grin.

Ms. Leon stopped talking and looked straight at Shelby. "It is very good of you to show such solidarity with your friends, Miss Trinity," she said, "even going so far as to want to share their detention. Admirable. Stupid, but admirable. Anyway, as I was saying . . ."

Shelby winced. It was not the first time that she had forgotten that Ms. Leon's hearing was considerably more acute than a human's. Nor would it be the first time that she and Laura shared a detention. Admittedly the previous occasion had involved the swimming pool, the senior boys' water polo team, and an electric eel, but at least that had been worth it.

"The first layer is a human one," Ms. Leon continued, "usually taking the form of button-operated silent alarms. In some ways this meeeww meeoow, mew mew . . . roooow?"

There were a couple of nervous giggles around the room as Ms. Leon tipped her head to one side with the closest thing to a look of confusion on her face that a cat could manage.

"Mew?" she meowed tentatively.

Laura noticed that the large blue gem in the center of the collar that Ms. Leon always wore was not illuminated.

Normally when she spoke, it was via the vocal synthesizer implanted in that collar, but now the crystal was dark. Laura raised her hand in the air, and Ms. Leon looked toward her and gave a small nod.

"Should I go and get the Professor, Ms. Leon?" Laura asked. Ms. Leon gave another, more emphatic, nod and Laura hurried out of the classroom and back toward the central computer core. As she ran down the corridor, she noticed that this part of the school was suddenly so cold that she could see her breath forming small white clouds.

The Professor looked up as she ran into the core. "Ah, Laura, there's just been another processor load spike," he said with a frown.

"Aye, I know, Professor. It's caused a wee problem," Laura said. She quickly recounted what had just happened in the stealth and evasion lesson.

"I should imagine Ms. Leon is not terribly happy," the Professor said, looking slightly nervous. Ms. Leon had never forgiven him for leaving her trapped in her new body, and the fact that he had thus far failed to find a way to reverse the process only made matters worse. In truth the stealth and evasion teacher had found unexpected advantages to her feline state, but she didn't intend to let the Professor know that.

"I think that's probably safe to say," Laura said as the Professor put down the display he'd been studying.

The pair of them hurried out of the core and back toward the stealth and evasion training area.

"I see that the environmental controls are malfunctioning too," the Professor said as they hurried down the corridor. If anything, it was even colder now than it had been just a minute before; a fine glittering layer of frost was just starting to form on the rock walls.

It became warmer again as they approached Ms. Leon's classroom, and they entered to find her prowling back and forth in an agitated way on the desk at the front of the room. As she saw the Professor, her eyes narrowed.

"Meeoow! Mew meewww rooow," she growled as they approached.

"I'm afraid we're experiencing some slight system problems," the Professor said as he examined the gem on her collar. "They appear to have interfered with the wireless connection between your vocal synthesizer and the network."

"Meeew meeeooow . . . you doddering old fool," Ms. Leon said, her eyes widening as the blue crystal flared back to life and her normal voice returned.

"Well . . . yes . . . um . . . Everything seems to be working again now," the Professor said with an embarrassed smile.

"Is this likely to happen again, Professor?" Ms. Leon asked quietly.

"It's . . . um . . . hard to say," the Professor said uncomfortably.

Ms. Leon raised a paw, a single curved claw sliding out from its sheath and pointing at him. The Professor swallowed nervously.

The cat spoke. "You had better hope it does not."

☢ ☢ ☢

Darkdoom looked up as Nero and Raven entered his office. Outside, night was just starting to fall over the Sydney skyline.

"Thank you for waiting," Diabolus said, gesturing at the two seats facing his desk. The other members of the ruling council had left an hour before. He needed to talk to these two alone.

"We cannot allow this to stand," Nero said as he sat down. "Trent has declared war."

"We cannot stop what we cannot find," Darkdoom said with a sigh. "Until we know where he is hiding, we can only sit and wait for him to make his next move. How close are you to tracking him down, Natalya?"

"Honestly, I am not sure," Raven replied. "Until we have analyzed the data on Khan's computer, it is impossible to say."

"Do you want my people to look at it?" Darkdoom asked.

"I would rather have Professor Pike do it," said Nero. "Under the circumstances, we cannot afford to take any chances that the data might be damaged during retrieval."

"Of course," Darkdoom agreed. "There's something else I need to discuss with you, though. You both know how much we owe Otto. He has done as much as anyone to ensure the survival of both H.I.V.E. and G.L.O.V.E. over the past couple of years, but that cannot be a reason to ignore the danger that he has now come to represent."

"I do not believe he has turned against us voluntarily," Nero said, frowning. "Trent must have done something to him, broken him somehow."

"I'm sure you're right," Darkdoom replied, "but that does not change the fact that he is now being used as a weapon against us. I want you both to know that I have not taken this decision lightly."

Nero recognized the look in his friend's eyes, and he did not like what it meant.

"I cannot ignore the feelings of the rest of the council in this matter," Darkdoom continued. "I'm afraid I have no alternative but to issue a capture or kill order."

"You can't do that," Nero said quickly. "You know as well as I do what that will mean to the other members of the council. You might as well issue a termination warrant."

"You saw what happened earlier, Max," Darkdoom snapped back. "If I don't act decisively now, there are those on the council who will simply see it as a sign of weakness. Do you really want someone like Chavez at the head of G.L.O.V.E.? You know he is just waiting for his chance to move against me."

"Give us more time," Raven said angrily. "That's all we need."

"I cannot, Natalya," Darkdoom replied, sounding frustrated. "What do you think will happen if another member of the council is assassinated? Chaos. There is a very real chance that it would mean the end of our organization. G.L.O.V.E. was founded on the principle that we were safer acting together than individually, but if Trent is allowed to pick us off one by one, this organization will implode. Without G.L.O.V.E., Trent will be completely unopposed, and the world will become a global police state or something far worse. I will not allow that to happen."

"We can stop him, Diabolus," Nero said. "There has to be another way."

"I wish there were, old friend," Diabolus said quietly. "I truly do."

"At least give me a head start," Raven said. "Twenty-four hours to analyze the data on the computer I retrieved. That's all I need."

"I'm afraid it's too late for that, Natalya," Darkdoom said with a sigh. "I gave the order ten minutes ago."

"You did what?" Nero snapped, suddenly furious.

"Otto's too dangerous, Max. You know that."

"Try telling that to your son when you have to explain to him how you ordered the execution of one of his friends!" Nero shouted. "If this is what being a member of this organization has come to mean, then it may very well be something that I, for one, no longer want to be a part of."

"Choose your next words very carefully, Max," Darkdoom said slowly.

"How dare you threaten me?" Nero said angrily, standing up. "Do I really need to tell you who you're starting to sound like?"

Suddenly the room was plunged into darkness, the only illumination coming from the lights of the city outside Darkdoom's office window.

"What the heck?" Darkdoom said, stabbing quickly at the communications console on his desk, but it too was dead.

A sudden tiny flicker caught Raven's eye, the briefest flash of bright red light flaring on the glass behind Darkdoom. She acted without hesitation, diving across Darkdoom's desk and knocking him to one side as the window pane behind him exploded. Diabolus grunted as the bullet struck him just below the shoulder blade, exiting through the front of his chest and spraying Raven's face with a fine mist of blood.

"Sniper!" Raven yelled at Nero. "Get down!"

Nero dived for cover just as another bullet tore into

the seat behind him. Raven hooked her arms under Darkdoom's shoulders, and he gave a low moan of pain as she crawled toward the door, struggling to drag his limp body.

"Get out of here!" Raven yelled as a bullet struck the wall half a yard above her head.

"Not without you," Nero said.

He crawled across the floor toward her and helped her drag Darkdoom the last few yards to the door. As Nero reached up and turned the door handle, another shot hit the door frame inches from his hand. Together he and Raven helped to haul Darkdoom out through the door just as a security guard came running down the corridor outside.

"Darkdoom's been hit," Nero yelled as the man in body armor approached.

"We've lost the security system building-wide," the guard reported. "It just shut down. No warning."

Nero had a horrible feeling that he knew what might have caused that to happen. "We have to get out of here NOW!" he snapped. "Natalya, take point. You"—he jabbed a finger at the guard—"help me with him."

The guard helped Nero lift Darkdoom, groaning, to his feet, one of the injured man's arms over each of their shoulders.

"We need to get to the roof," Raven said, looking down the corridor.

"The hangar bay is locked down," the guard replied. "The only way out is at ground level."

The corridor was suddenly filled with a bloodred glow as the emergency lighting kicked on.

"No. That's where they want us," Raven said quickly. "We have to get to the Shroud."

"I just told you, it's sealed tight," the guard said, looking confused. "We can't get in."

"I'll find a way," said Raven, drawing the crackling purple blades from the twin sheaths on her back. "Where are the stairs?"

"That way," the guard said, pointing down the corridor.

They set off, Raven in the lead, Nero and the guard behind, carrying Darkdoom between them.

As they passed the elevators, the guard noticed that the call buttons beside the doors were illuminated.

"We can take the elevator," the guard said. "It'd be quicker."

"Trust me," Raven said, shaking her head slightly, "not a good idea."

☺ ☺ ☺

Otto walked into the security control center on the ground floor of the building flanked by two men in full body armor and carrying assault rifles. Their chests displayed an image of an angel flying upward with a sword held aloft in its outstretched hand. The symbol of H.O.P.E.

The leader of the three-man team that had gone into the room before them pushed the dead body of the G.L.O.V.E. security technician out of his chair in front of the numerous security monitors. Otto walked over, sat in the recently vacated seat, and began to study the displays.

He could see G.L.O.V.E. security guards hurrying to their positions throughout the upper floors of the building, but they weren't what he was looking for. He eventually spotted movement on a monitor in the upper left corner of the array and realized that he'd found his targets. Captured on the screen were several familiar faces. He reached for the transmit button on his comms unit and was about to relay the position of the fleeing group when he suddenly felt a sharp pain in his head. He sucked a quick involuntary breath through his teeth as the pain intensified. He knew that he had to report the position of the targets, but something was stopping him from speaking. He fought against the block, knowing what he was supposed to do, but still he couldn't speak. It was as if somewhere inside his head a tiny voice were screaming at him to ignore orders, to let them get away. He took a long deep breath and forced himself to focus. Then he pressed the button and spoke.

"All units, targets are heading to the roof via the east stairwell."

"Roger that," Ghost's voice said in his earpiece. "Moving to intercept."

☺ ☺ ☺

Raven looked down the gap between the guardrails around the concrete staircase as she heard the sound of raised voices from several floors below. Heavily armed men were pouring into the stairwell, a couple of them looking upward to spot their fleeing quarry.

"Keep moving," she growled at Nero and the lone G.L.O.V.E. guard, who were struggling to carry their injured burden toward the door at the top of the stairs. As they approached the door, Raven pushed past them and opened it, popping her head through the doorway to check that the corridor beyond was clear. Seeing nothing, she beckoned the other two forward.

"Get to the hangar doors. I'll be right behind you," she said quickly. As the door closed behind the two men, she looked back down the stairwell. Their pursuers were now just a couple of floors below her. Too close. She detached one of the two small cylinders that were strapped to the tactical webbing on the left side of her chest, popped off the small protective cap with her thumb, and pressed the stud on top. She waited for two interminable seconds and then dropped the metal tube, already turning to run as it tumbled through the seemingly bottomless void in the center of the stairwell. As it passed the level of the pursuing H.O.P.E. assault team, it detonated with an enormous bang and a bright white flash of light. The few men on the stairs who had been wearing night vision goggles were blinded instantly, perhaps permanently. The others were stunned by the concussive force of the explosion and were sent reeling, their hands covering their damaged ears.

As Raven ran down the corridor toward the hangar doors, she knew that she had bought them only thirty seconds, a minute at most. More worrying was the fact that Darkdoom was no longer even groaning. He had gone silent, and his skin was pale and clammy. If they could get him to the Shroud, she could try to stabilize him, but he was losing too much blood. She only needed to look at the crimson trail that he was leaving on the ground to see that.

They reached the heavy steel doors that sealed off the hangar, and Raven stabbed at the button that would normally open them, unsurprised by the lack of response. She hit the switch on the hilt of one of her swords and configured the variable geometry force field along its blade to the sharpest possible cutting edge. She pressed the tip of the blade to the cold metal of the door and pushed, the crackling point of the sword sinking into the toughened metal with ease. She pulled downward firmly, the blade sliding through the steel with a hum, the metal of the door glowing white hot along the thin line she was carving. Raven finished the first cut and proceeded to make another one, forming a low rectangle. She pulled the sword out again, sliding it into the scabbard on her back, and gave the door a solid kick. The weakened section fell into the room beyond with a loud clang, and Raven watched as Nero and the security guard carefully maneuvered Darkdoom through. She glanced back down the corridor as she followed them, and saw the H.O.P.E. assault team pouring out of the stairwell and into the corridor just thirty yards away.

"Go! Get to the Shroud," she yelled to Nero, pulling the last flash-bang grenade from her harness and tossing it back through the hole in the door. She heard it detonate as she ran across the hangar toward the waiting Shroud, the drop ship's engines spinning up with a high-pitched whine. Above her was nothing but the dark night sky; clearly whatever had disabled the security system had also deactivated the holographic field concealing the landing pad.

Suddenly a masked figure in gleaming white body armor dropped to the hangar floor from somewhere overhead, blocking Raven's route to the Shroud.

"Going somewhere?" Ghost asked.

"Yes. Through you," Raven replied, drawing the twin swords from her back.

"I've been waiting a long time for this," Ghost said.

Raven struck, aiming a sweeping blow at the other woman's head, but Ghost blocked the blow with her forearm. The sword struck the armor plate with a crackle, but did no damage. Ghost struck back, the straight edge of her hand snaking out and hitting Raven in the wrist, paralyzing her hand so that the sword dropped from her numb fingers. Ghost followed up with a flat-palmed blow to Raven's chest that sent her staggering backward. Raven fought to take a breath while ignoring the sharp pain. The last time she had been hit that hard and that fast had been when she'd been fighting Cypher's robotic assassins.

"I'm going to take you apart piece by piece," Ghost said. It was impossible to tell through her smooth white faceplate, but Raven felt sure that the other woman was smiling. Ghost flicked her wrists, and triangular black blades shot out from beneath the armor on her forearms.

Raven backed away. She could hear the rest of the H.O.P.E. soldiers pouring into the hangar somewhere behind her. Ghost raised a single hand, ordering them to hold position as she advanced toward Raven again. She struck impossibly quickly. Raven barely had time to raise a katana to block the killing blow aimed at her neck, deflecting Ghost's wrist blade just enough that it only opened a gash in her shoulder. Raven winced and struck back, but her blade bounced ineffectually off her opponent's armored chest plate.

"You can't win," Ghost said, and kicked at Raven's thigh. Raven gasped in pain, dropping to one knee and raising her sword to block Ghost's blade as it swung toward her again. Ghost pushed downward, forcing Raven's sparking blade back toward her own face. Raven pushed with all her strength, but the other woman was impossibly strong, and Raven could feel the power draining from her arm as the blade moved closer and closer.

"Hey!"

Raven glanced past Ghost and saw Nero standing at the bottom of the Shroud's loading ramp, a large pistol leveled straight at Ghost. Raven felt the pressure on her sword ease the tiniest amount as Ghost turned her head to face the Shroud. Nero pulled the trigger, and the flare gun fired, the hissing red ball of fire shooting across the hangar and striking Ghost's faceplate. Ghost staggered backward, and Raven leaped to her feet, running for the drop ship.

"Kill them!" Ghost yelled at the H.O.P.E. assault team, her hands covering her face.

Raven ignored the bullets that whizzed past her as she raced up the ramp into the Shroud's cargo bay.

"GO!" Nero yelled over his shoulder as he slapped at the button that closed the boarding ramp. Up on the flight deck the pilot maxed out the throttle, the Shroud's engines roaring as it shot up out of the hangar.

Ghost watched from the hangar floor as the Shroud lifted up into the night sky.

"Targets are in flight," she said calmly.

$$\odot\ \odot\ \odot$$

Otto looked up from the pavement outside the G.L.O.V.E. building, watching the Shroud climbing into the sky.

"Now, Malpense," Trent's voice crackled in his ear, "bring them down."

Otto reached out with his senses, feeling for the flight control computers on board the fleeing aircraft. He could feel the systems he wanted, and he did not need long. He twitched his head slightly, and the Shroud veered off course, straight toward a nearby building, its manual controls locked out and its throttle jammed at full thrust.

The sudden pain in Otto's head came from nowhere, a searing agony that broke his concentration and released the systems on board the Shroud. Otto dropped to his knees, screaming and clutching his head as black Animus fluid trickled from his nose. He gave one final gasp and then tipped forward, hitting the pavement with a thud, unconscious.

On board the Shroud the pilot swore under his breath and wrenched at the controls, pulling on the joystick and banking the Shroud hard to the right. The left engine housing smashed through the plate glass of one of the corner offices in the building that they had been on a direct collision course with just seconds earlier. The Shroud bucked with the impact. The pilot fought to bring the aircraft back under control, leveling out and scanning his control panel for warning lights before steering toward clear sky and engaging the cloaking field with a relieved sigh.

"What happened there?" Nero asked as he climbed up to the flight deck.

"I have no idea," the pilot said, his face a mix of confusion and relief. "I had a dead stick for a few seconds, and we almost hit a building. I've never seen anything like it. It was like the damn thing was trying to crash itself."

Nero thought back to the fate that had met Jonas Steiner's private jet and realized he knew what might have caused that to happen.

"Get us back to H.I.V.E. as fast as possible," he said. "We have to get Darkdoom to the medical facility." Nero knew that there were hospitals closer than H.I.V.E., but taking Darkdoom to one of them would be suicide. H.O.P.E. was sure to be watching and waiting for them to do exactly that.

"ETA is just under two hours from now," the pilot said, "and that's red-lining it all the way."

"Understood," Nero replied. He just prayed that would be fast enough.

He climbed back down into the Shroud's passenger compartment, where Raven was fighting to stabilize Darkdoom's condition. Her hands were covered in blood and she was struggling to get an IV line into the wounded man's arm.

"Is he going to survive?" Nero asked.

"I've done all I can here," Raven replied, shaking her head slightly. "It doesn't look good, Max."

"We'll be back at H.I.V.E. in less than two hours," Nero said. "The medical team will be waiting on the pad."

"I'm not sure he has that long." She wiped her forehead with the back of her hand. "He's lost a lot of blood."

"He's strong, Natalya," Nero said, placing a hand on her arm. "If anyone has the sheer will to survive, it's him. How are you?" Nero asked, gesturing at the deep gash in her shoulder.

"I'll live," Raven replied. "Whoever that woman was, she is as capable as anyone I've ever encountered. I don't think I could have stopped her without your help. Her armor was immune to my blades, and . . . well . . . I just wasn't strong enough."

"You have been on a tough assignment for weeks and

just survived an assassination attempt," Nero said, shaking his head. "Don't be too hard on yourself."

"That is no excuse," Raven said, frowning. "Next time I will be better prepared."

"Regardless, that is not our most serious problem," Nero said.

"What do you mean?"

"The failure of the security system, the hijacking of the Shroud's flight control systems, the very fact that H.O.P.E. knew exactly when and where to hit us. . . . I'm afraid it all points to one thing."

"Otto," Raven said quietly. "You think he was there."

"I'm sure of it," Nero said, sounding suddenly tired. "I'm afraid it just highlights what a danger to us he has become."

"It still does not justify what Diabolus did," Raven replied. "You know as well as I do that the order he gave cannot be countermanded. Every G.L.O.V.E. kill team on the planet will be looking for him now."

"Which is why we have to find him first," Nero said with a sigh.

chapter four

Laura stared at the display on the desk. Shelby had gone to bed an hour before, but Laura knew she'd find it impossible to sleep with the mystery rattling around inside her head of what was causing the systems malfunctions. It made no sense that the network's storage capacity was dropping but no new data was taking up that space. She tapped at the keyboard, pulling up another screen of diagnostics. She knew that the strange events had started a few months ago, so she started to run a byte by byte comparison of all the files on the system from that approximate date forward. She was not surprised to find that many of the file sizes had changed over that period, but suddenly something struck her as odd. Of the huge number of archived files that she did not have the right permission to access, at least some were showing file size mismatches that made no sense. These were old files, files that had apparently not been called up in years, and yet some of them were showing tiny increases in size. These were the ones that caught her attention. All she could do was pull the dates on which they'd last been modified. Almost immediately she started to see a pattern emerge. The tiny increases in file size had happened at the exact same times as the system glitches. She checked again, wanting to be sure of what she'd found.

Laura got up and hit the button to leave the room, but the buzz from the door quickly reminded her that the accommodation blocks were in nighttime lockdown. She pulled her Blackbox communicator from the pocket of her jumpsuit and placed a call to Professor Pike. The screen flashed the single word "connecting" for a few seconds, and then the Professor's face appeared on the screen. From what she could see of the background, he was still in the computer core.

"It's very late, Miss Brand. I hope this is something important," the Professor said.

"Aye, Professor, I think it might be," Laura said. "I think I know where our phantom data is hiding."

☣ ☣ ☣

The Shroud touched down in H.I.V.E.'s crater landing bay, and the medical team that had been waiting at the edge of the pad rushed forward as the engines spun to a halt. Nero hurried down the landing ramp at the rear of the aircraft and ushered the team to the craft. Barely a minute later the medics wheeled a gurney back down the ramp with Darkdoom's pale, unconscious body on it. Dr. Scott, H.I.V.E.'s chief medical officer, walked alongside the stretcher, looking at a portable screen that was displaying the wounded man's vitals. Judging by his face, the doctor was not happy with what he saw.

"Prep him for immediate surgery," he said.

Nero walked back down the Shroud's ramp and watched the medical team leave, knowing that now was not the time to interfere.

"He's in good hands, Max," Raven said.

"I know," Nero replied, "but that's not all I'm worried about."

"What do you mean?" she asked.

"Word of the attack on Diabolus is bound to leak out. You saw what the atmosphere was like in the council meeting. The one thing that G.L.O.V.E. does not need now is a power vacuum, and I fear that Trent is perfectly aware of that."

"You think that the council will move to replace him?"

"It is not beyond the realm of possibility," Nero said with a sigh. "They are a group of people not known for their patience, and I fear that some among the council will see this as a perfect opportunity to stake their claim."

Raven did not want to believe that was true, but, then, she had never been particularly interested in the politics and power games that the senior members of G.L.O.V.E. got up to behind the scenes. She was more the practical problem-solving—or, more accurately, problem-eliminating—type.

Nero saw Professor Pike and Laura Brand hurrying across the landing pad toward them, and he tried to put to one side his concerns over Diabolus's condition and what it meant for G.L.O.V.E. He had a school to run too.

"Professor, Miss Brand," Nero said with a nod of acknowledgment as they approached, "is there something I can do for you?"

"I believe Laura has made a breakthrough in solving what is going wrong with the school's systems," the Professor said quickly.

"I see," Nero said. "Is it something that can wait until the morning?" Nero would never admit it in front of one of his pupils, but it had been a very long day and he needed to get at least a few hours' sleep. An aura of inhuman endurance could be a difficult thing to maintain at times.

"No, I don't think it can," Professor Pike said, shaking his head. "We may be running out of time."

� ☁ ☁

"What happened?" Trent said angrily, looking through the thick glass at the technicians and medics gathered around Otto's unconscious body.

"We're not sure," Dr. Creed replied nervously. "His biometric readings looked fine, and then suddenly his neural activity went off the charts. A few moments later the Animus fluid became temporarily inert, almost as if it were shut down."

"You assured me that Animus was immune to these sorts of problems," Trent replied, sounding impatient.

"It is—well, it should be," Creed replied. "We know that Animus was probably conceived as an organic computer system that would be immune to any form of electronic disruption, specifically the electromagnetic pulse that accompanies a nuclear detonation. That's the beauty of an organic supercomputer. It is self-replicating and self-repairing. In theory, even if only a tiny amount of the fluid survives an attempt to destroy it, the whole system will be able to rebuild itself. I would love to meet its original designer."

"I'm afraid that will not be possible. He died some time ago," Trent replied.

"The nanotechnology alone is a quantum leap ahead of anything anyone else has been able to achieve. We are still years away from being able to create nanites that allow even limited movement or such rapid replication. With it as fully integrated and in the boy's nervous system as it is now, he should be entirely subject to our control . . . programmable."

"I know all of this, Doctor, and none of it explains what happened today," Trent said. "The boy is too valuable an asset for this sort of failure. I need to be sure that he is reliable."

"I understand," Creed replied. "Rest assured that my team and I will be working around the clock to fix this."

"See that you do," Trent said coldly. "No mistakes, Creed. You would be a difficult, but not impossible, man to replace."

"Yes . . . sir," Creed replied, swallowing nervously.

Trent walked out of the medical bay with an irritated scowl on his face. The Malpense boy had to be operating at full efficiency. It was essential if he was going to continue with his mission to eliminate G.L.O.V.E. Without him they lost their penetration of G.L.O.V.E.'s communication network, which would make locating their targets next to impossible, given that they were a group of people who had made careers out of being difficult to find.

Ghost was waiting just outside the door and fell into step alongside Trent as he stalked away down the corridor.

"Do they know what caused the boy to go off-mission yet?" she asked as they walked.

"No, but Creed assures me that it's only a matter of time before they do," Trent said. "I take it that you experienced no such problems."

"My implants functioned perfectly," she replied, "but it would not have mattered that Malpense did not carry out his mission correctly if I had succeeded in mine."

"Nero was never going to be an easy target, especially with his trained attack dog in tow," Trent pointed out.

"I had her," Ghost said, the frustration clear in her voice. "I would have finished her if it had not been for Nero's intervention."

"Of course you would," Trent agreed. "That is, after all, what you were designed to do."

"She will not be so lucky next time," said Ghost, her hands clenching into fists.

"I need to make a call," Trent said as they approached the door to his office. "You should start preparations for your next mission. I want to move as soon as Malpense has located our next target."

Ghost gave a quick nod and strode away down the corridor. Trent smiled slightly. The truth of the matter was that he had been extremely pleased with her performance in Sydney. Despite the enhancements to her body, he had still had his doubts about whether it would be enough when she confronted someone as lethal and ruthless as Raven. As it was, she had exceeded his expectations, which was considerably more than he could say for Malpense.

He walked into his office and sat down at his desk. There was no decoration, in accordance with his usual tastes—just plain concrete walls and a single metal desk with a secure terminal. It was all he needed. He keyed in his encryption code and connected to the secure comms line. After a few seconds three digitally distorted faces appeared on the screen in front of him.

"We have studied your report on the operation in Australia," the man on the left said. "A disappointing result."

"Yes," Trent replied, "but if Darkdoom isn't already dead, he will at least be out of action for some time. His condition should serve to further increase the chaos within G.L.O.V.E. This is just a temporary setback. We should not lose sight of our long-term goals."

"That may well be," the woman on the right said, "but those long-term goals are dependent on the Malpense boy being a reliable asset. His failure on this mission is . . . troubling."

"You may assure the rest of the Disciples that we are urgently investigating the causes of his current condition. Dr. Creed assures me that he will soon have answers."

"The project depends on that," the man in the center of the screen said. "If we truly are to honor the legacy of this group's founder, we cannot afford any mistakes."

"I understand," Trent replied. "I will keep you apprised of the boy's condition. In the meantime I will divert all of H.O.P.E.'s resources to finding whatever rock Nero and Darkdoom have crawled under."

"It is somewhat frustrating that we have not yet been able to determine the precise location of the school," the woman on the screen said.

"Nero has gone to an extraordinary amount of trouble to keep that facility hidden," Trent replied. "It is his greatest vulnerability, so it is perhaps not surprising that he has gone to such lengths. From what we have been able to determine, it would appear that not even the members of G.L.O.V.E.'s ruling council know exactly where it is."

"Surely Malpense must have some clue as to its location," the man on the left said.

"Perhaps, but the Animus fluid keeps his conscious personality suppressed. To interrogate him I would have to reverse the process that allows us to control him. Doing that would be traumatic, perhaps even lethal. We all know he is too valuable for that."

"So, what is the next step?" the woman asked.

"We continue with the disassembly of G.L.O.V.E. until Nero or Darkdoom breaks cover," Trent replied.

"Agreed," the man on the left said.

"Of course," the woman on the right agreed.

"Let us hope we do not suffer any more unforeseen setbacks," the man in the center said.

"Do not worry," Trent said with a smile. "G.L.O.V.E. is finished. It's only a matter of time."

"So tell me, Professor," Nero said with a tired sigh, "what is so urgent that it could not wait until the morning?"

"I believe we may have found what has been causing the problems with H.I.V.E.'s systems," the Professor said, looking anxious.

"Really?" Nero said. "I take it that it is something I need to be concerned about."

"Yes," the Professor replied. "I'm afraid an aggressive program appears to be attempting to build new code within our system. Miss Brand has found sections of code very well hidden within the network, very well hidden indeed. The problem we have now is that neither she nor I can determine exactly what it's designed to do or who is responsible for concealing its presence in such a devious way."

"Is it a virus?" Nero asked, secretly hoping that this would be one of the occasions when the Professor explained things without going into too much technical detail.

"Not really," Laura said. "A virus is usually designed simply to replicate itself, to spread, just like an organic virus. This almost seems like something is being constructed from scratch. It's not making copies of itself; it's growing."

"I'm afraid the distinction is rather lost on me, Miss Brand," Nero said, sounding slightly impatient. "I assume that it is something hostile, judging by the disruption it has been causing. Certainly we need to stop it before it can do serious, lasting harm. Thus far it has been little more than an inconvenience. I do not wish to wait until it becomes something more sinister. Can you remove it?"

"That's the most worrying thing," the Professor said with a frown. "We've tried to, but every time we remove any of the mystery data, it simply reappears somewhere else on the system. If I did not know better, I would say that it's behaving intelligently."

Nero felt a sudden cold chill run down his spine.

"Are you saying that the code in question is aware of what you're trying to do?" he asked.

"It rather appears that way, yes," the Professor replied. "The code being built is more complex than anything either I or Miss Brand have ever seen before. I may have had a hand in designing artificial-intelligence systems in the past, but I was merely building upon the work of others. This is all rather beyond my experience."

"I see," Nero said, rubbing the bridge of his nose. "Thank you for your work on this, Miss Brand. You appear to have been most helpful. I think you should return to the accommodation block now. It's very late and you have classes tomorrow."

"But, sir, I—," Laura began.

"It was not a request, Miss Brand," Nero said calmly. "I

am sure that the Professor will keep you updated on any developments."

Laura looked for a moment like she might be going to argue, but then thought better of it.

"Yes, sir," she replied with a sigh before leaving Nero's office.

"I do not like the sound of this, Professor," Nero said as the door closed behind her. "What's our next step?"

"Well, what we really need is an expert in designing and controlling AIs, and no one on the island has that kind of experience," the Professor replied with a frown.

"Actually, Professor," said Nero, looking slightly uncomfortable, "that is not strictly true."

☢ ☢ ☢

"Dr. Creed," the young technician sitting at a nearby workstation said, "I think I've found something."

"What is it?" Creed said, walking behind her and peering over her shoulder at the display.

"Here," the tech said, pointing at the three-dimensional image of a brain on the screen, "near the stem. It's so small and well concealed that we missed it during earlier scans."

"What is it?" Creed asked, examining the tiny ovoid deformation in the normal structure of the brain.

"I have no idea," the technician replied honestly. "It appears to be organic, but it also seems to be shielded somehow from our normal scanning techniques. I've never seen anything quite like it."

"Curious," Creed said, frowning. "Can we remove it?"

"Not without killing the boy," the technician replied. "It's fully integrated with his brain tissue, almost as if it's a natural structure. That's probably why we missed it during our earlier scans. If it is artificial, then someone has gone to extraordinary lengths to conceal it and to ensure that it cannot be tampered with."

"Overlay the scan of Animus penetration of the brain tissue," Creed said, and the technician typed a series of commands that displayed a new layer on top of the original image. This new layer displayed a veiny black web that seemed to have penetrated every cubic inch of the brain tissue. Everywhere except for one small area—the exact same area that the mysterious object occupied.

"There," Creed said. "See how the Animus has penetrated completely throughout the cerebellum but has avoided that area."

"Why would that be?" the technician asked, sounding confused.

"Your guess is as good as mine," Creed replied. "Let's try something," he went on. "Activate real-time scanning and give the Animus explicit instructions to attempt integration with the object."

"It'll take a couple of minutes," the technician said as

she started to tap away at her keyboard.

"There," she said eventually. "Bringing up real-time scan."

The display changed to a zoomed-in view of the Animus penetration around the object, as several of the tendrils of the black fluid crept toward it. Creed's eyes widened as just a moment later he saw the Animus shrink away from the object. It was impossible to say whether it had been driven back or had recoiled voluntarily, but the reason was at least clear why this tiny part of Malpense's brain had remained free of Animus. Unfortunately, it left them no closer to understanding what the object was. That would require an invasive, almost certainly fatal surgical procedure, and Creed knew there was no way that Trent would authorize that.

"Neural activity is increasing," a technician on the other side of the lab reported. "I think he's waking up."

"Excellent," Dr. Creed replied. He did not know if their attempt to force the Animus to integrate with the mysterious object was related to Malpense's sudden revival, but it seemed like rather a coincidence.

The doctor walked over to the bed in the center of the lab and looked down at the boy as his Animus-darkened eyes flickered open.

"Welcome back, Mr. Malpense," Creed said as the boy focused on him. "I trust you are feeling better."

"What happened?" Otto asked, his voice croaky.

"You suffered a period of unconsciousness during your last mission," Creed replied. "You have been asleep for some time."

"Did the targets escape?" Otto asked, frowning.

"Yes, I'm afraid they did," Creed replied.

"It will not happen again," Otto said, looking suddenly angry. "Such weakness is unacceptable."

He sat up and swung his legs over the side of the bed.

"Not so fast, Mr. Malpense," Creed replied. "I have some tests to run before I pass you as mission fit again."

"Then, get on with it," Otto said impatiently. "I want to get back to my work."

"Of course you do," Creed replied with a faint smile.

Otto lay back down on the bed as various technicians busied themselves with analyzing his mental and physical condition. As the work continued, Creed observed the boy and saw that his eyes followed everything. Creed had seen many bizarre and chilling things over the course of his career working for H.O.P.E., but there was still something about this young subject that he found deeply unsettling. He knew that he would have to report all the details of the boy's condition to Trent, including their discovery of the strange object hidden deep within his brain. Creed also knew that Trent would be less than satisfied with his inability to explain its purpose and origins.

☻ ☻ ☻

Raven watched the painstaking and delicate work of the surgical team through the observation window. They had already been working on Darkdoom for the best part of an hour. She knew it was foolish to blame herself for his condition. Indeed, she'd almost certainly saved his life. The sniper in Sydney had been going for a head shot, and only her swift action had prevented his instant death. That, however, was not the way her mind worked. Instead she found herself wondering what would have happened if she had moved just a fraction of a second faster, reacted slightly more quickly.

One of the surgeons made her way out of the theatre, pulling off her blood-smeared latex gloves and removing her surgical mask as she walked over to where Raven was standing.

"How is he, Doctor?" Raven asked as the woman approached, not taking her eyes off the scene beyond the glass.

"It is too soon to say," the doctor replied. "He has a collapsed lung, and the bullet grazed his heart. He lost a lot of blood on the journey. It would have been better to have taken him to the nearest hospital instead of bringing him here."

"That was not an option." Raven's voice was calm.

"I'll take your word for it. Still, you did a good job of stabilizing his condition. You probably saved his life."

"I think it is perhaps a little too early for congratulations," Raven said with a sigh. It was not the first time that she had been grateful for the emergency medical training she had received as part of her schooling so many years before.

"Let me look at that," the doctor said, gesturing toward the deep cut left in Raven's shoulder by Ghost's wrist blade.

Raven shrugged. "It's just a scratch. You have more pressing concerns."

"Dr. Scott does not need my assistance with this stage of the surgery," the doctor replied, "and scratches do not, generally speaking, look like they need quite so many stitches."

"Maybe later, Doctor," Raven said, picking up Khan's laptop from the seat behind her. "I need to get this to Professor Pike now. It may provide us with a clue that will help us find the people who did this."

If it did, the best medical care in the world would not be able to save them. She intended to make quite sure of that.

☣ ☣ ☣

The black limousine pulled into the abandoned warehouse, and several men in dark suits got out. They were all carrying compact submachine guns, and they scanned their surroundings with practiced efficiency. The driver of the car walked to the car's rear door and opened it, giving a courteous nod to Lin Feng as he stepped out.

"I'm glad you could make it," Carlos Chavez said, emerging from the shadows nearby, flanked by two of his own guards.

"I am not sure it is wise for us to meet like this under the current circumstances," said Lin Feng. "I assume that you have heard about the attack on Darkdoom."

"Yes," Chavez said. "That is part of the reason I wanted to see you. I think that we need to discuss exactly what this means for G.L.O.V.E." He gestured for Lin Feng to follow him a short distance away so that their conversation would not be overheard. They both knew just how dangerous it would be if someone unsympathetic to their position were to learn of this conversation.

"Go on," Lin Feng invited, unwilling to be the first to lay his cards on the table.

"I would not want to assume too much, but I am fairly sure that I am not the only one who has become unhappy with Darkdoom's leadership," Chavez said quietly.

"If the rumors are to be believed, that is a situation that may not be of concern for very much longer," Lin Feng replied. "Indeed, it may already be time to start to consider who should replace him."

Chavez looked at Lin Feng, trying to see what the other man was thinking. "I, for one, do not think that we can afford to wait and see how this plays out," he said carefully. "With H.O.P.E. coming after us all so aggressively, we must have strong leadership at all times."

"I take it you have an alternative suggestion?" Lin Feng said quietly.

"That is why I wanted to meet with you," Chavez replied. "I need to know if I would have your support if I were to put myself forward as a candidate."

"I see," Lin Feng said. The truth was that it was exactly what he had wanted to hear. Chavez had climbed to power in his own region through a combination of brutality and low animal cunning, and while that might be enough to ensure his place on the council, it did not mark him out as someone with the finesse required to run G.L.O.V.E. But that was precisely what made Chavez so useful. This fool could act as Lin Feng's stalking horse, drawing the fire of the other members of the ruling council. He would let Chavez make his clumsy bid for power, and when the dust had settled from the chaos that would inevitably follow, he—Lin Feng—would step in and pick up the pieces.

"I would not object to such a suggestion," Lin Feng continued, "but you know as well as I do that Nero would never tolerate it."

"Nero has his own problems," Chavez said impatiently. "If it were not for the fact that he cannot even control his own students, we would not be in this situation in the first place."

"It would be a serious mistake to underestimate him," Lin Feng replied. "Even with the problems he currently faces, he is not the sort of man you want as an opponent."

"I know that," Chavez said, "which is exactly why we need to weaken his position."

"And how exactly would you hope to do that?" asked Lin Feng, raising an eyebrow.

"By exploiting his greatest weakness. Darkdoom's capture or kill order still stands. Regardless of his current condition, he is still the only person who can countermand it. Nero will go to any lengths to retrieve the Malpense boy without harming him. We, however, are under no such restrictions. If we can eliminate Malpense before Nero can mount a rescue attempt, we will seriously undermine his credibility with the council, while simultaneously strengthening our own."

"Or we may wake one morning to find Raven standing over us," Lin Feng replied.

"Which is why, before we do anything else, we need to remove that particular piece from the board," Chavez said.

"Eliminate Raven? Easier said than done."

"But not impossible," Chavez said with a small smile.

chapter five

Laura groaned as the morning alarm buzzer went off in her and Shelby's quarters. She'd managed to get only four hours' sleep after her late-night meeting with Nero and the Professor, and the full day of lessons that loomed before her was not a pleasant prospect. Shelby walked out of the bathroom at the rear of the room, toweling her hair dry and already wearing her black Alpha stream jumpsuit.

"You look like death," Shelby said cheerily as Laura reluctantly climbed out of bed.

"Thanks for that," she groaned.

"So where'd you get to last night?" Shelby asked.

"I made a bit of a breakthrough with tracking down the source of the gremlins in the school's systems," Laura said, rubbing the back of her neck. "I had to update the Professor."

"You get it fixed?" Shelby asked, hoping for a short answer.

"No, not yet," Laura replied, "but we're getting there."

The truth was that Laura really wasn't sure how much they had achieved with such a limited understanding of exactly what was behind the problem.

"You better get a move on," Shelby said with a grin as Laura slowly shuffled toward the bathroom. "Who knows what'll be left if Franz hits the breakfast buffet before we do? You'll need to eat something. We've got political corruption class this morning."

Laura groaned again. As she walked into the bathroom, the door hissed shut behind her. Shelby was busy doing her hair in the mirror when she heard a startled shriek. "Still not fixed the showers, then," she said with a grin.

☺☺☺

"Did you find anything?" Raven asked as she walked into the cluttered workshop at the rear of the science and technology classroom.

The Professor looked up from the laptop on the workbench in front of him and stared at Raven for a moment like he didn't know who she was. A moment later he seemed to zone back in and focus on her properly.

"I'm sorry," the Professor said with a slight frown. "What was that?"

"The laptop—did you find anything on it?" Raven said, gesturing at the computer.

"Oh, yes, but it was quite well protected." He pulled a small square of gray puttylike material from the pocket of his lab coat. "Though I think that much C4 is rather excessive. It was rigged to blow on the third incorrect password entry. That would have made retrieval of any data from the hard drive problematic. Heaven only knows what you're supposed to do if you're a poor typist." He slipped the explosive back into his pocket.

Raven was suddenly rather glad that she had not tried to hack into the machine herself. Khan might have been paranoid, but you had to admire his dedication to computer security. There had been enough explosive concealed inside the laptop to destroy a tank.

"Anyway, it's quite safe now," the Professor continued. "I've just been looking at the first few files that seem relevant to what you're searching for."

Raven stepped behind him and looked over his shoulder at the display. On the screen were a number of architectural drawings. She was no expert, but the lack of any exterior windows suggested that the facility was probably hidden belowground.

"It looks like a fairly standard operations base," Raven said, frowning. "You could build that anywhere. We need something that gives us a locational clue. Is there anything like that?"

"Nothing immediately obvious," the Professor said with a frown. "Hold on. What's this?"

He opened another file, and inside was a series of images of scanned receipts for construction materials. All the scans had large black blocks obscuring any indication of where the materials in question had been ordered from or were delivered to. Khan had gone to great lengths to ensure that nobody would be able to identify the location of the facility easily. The Professor continued to scroll through the images, hoping that one might have been missed or that there might be some other clue that would give them an indication of where Trent was hiding.

"Stop," Raven said. "Go back."

The Professor pulled up the image that he had gone past a few moments before.

"There," Raven said, pointing at the screen. "What's that?"

Just visible at the edge of the scanned document was a tiny mark. It looked like something had been trapped on the glass of the scanner when the image had been originally been captured. The Professor centered the screen on the object and zoomed in. The tiny speck became a blurry black blob. He quickly tapped at the keyboard, and the resolution improved tenfold. Now they could both make out a distinctive organic shape to the object.

"What is it?" Raven asked.

"Some kind of spore or seed, by the looks of it," the Professor said, examining the image carefully. "If I were you, I'd show it to Ms. Gonzales. She might be able to tell you more." Ms. Gonzales was the head of H.I.V.E.'s biotechnology department and an expert on all kinds of plants. "I'll copy it to a thumb drive for you."

The Professor quickly inserted a compact memory stick into the port on the side of the laptop and copied the image onto it before handing it to Raven.

"Do you really think this might help with finding Otto?" the Professor asked as Raven turned to leave.

"I don't know," Raven replied, "but it's the only lead we've got."

☹ ☹ ☹

"Are you okay?" Wing asked as Laura sat down at the table in the dining hall.

"If one more person asks me that, I'm going to smack them in the mouth," Laura said irritably.

"Ignore the grumpy Scot," Shelby said with a grin as she sat down next to her. "She didn't get much sleep last night."

"Coding into the wee small hours again?" Lucy asked as she took a seat on the other side of Laura.

"Actually, no," Laura said. "I was trying to help sort out the gremlins in the school's systems. I can give you all the technical details if you want."

"No," all three of the others said in perfect unison.

"Luddites," Laura said with a slight smile. Otto would have wanted to know every last detail. Just one more reason why she missed having him around.

"Morning," Nigel said, sitting down with his breakfast tray. "Gosh, Laura, you look terrible."

Shelby placed a calming hand on Laura's wrist as she saw the knuckles on Laura's clenched fist whiten. Franz sat down next to Nigel with a rather confused look on his face.

"I am thinking I must be seeing things," Franz said. "I am walking past Block and Tackle just now, and they are . . . well . . . hugging each other."

Laura gave a quick snort of laughter.

"I thought you said it would wear off in a couple of hours," she said, grinning at Lucy.

"Well, it kinda depends on how intelligent the individual is, so . . ."

"What did you do?" Shelby asked, looking from one to the other with a raised eyebrow. Laura quickly recounted the details of her encounter with the two bullies the previous day.

"Awwww, that's so sweet," Shelby said with a broad grin. "Young love."

"A truly horrifying mental image has just formed in my head," Wing said with a frown. "I am only glad that I did not have to witness in person what you have just described."

"Do you think you could use that voice of yours to give tall, dark, and handsome here a sense of humor?" Shelby asked Lucy with a grin.

"There are limits to even my powers," Lucy replied with a chuckle.

"I suspect that I am once again being mocked," Wing said, the tiniest of smiles tugging at one corner of his mouth.

"You know we all love you just the way you are, Spock," Shelby said quickly, and Laura and Lucy both started laughing at Wing's slightly wounded expression.

All six of them were still laughing and joking as Dr. Nero walked up to the table with a serious expression.

"Nigel, could you come with me, please?" Nero asked quietly.

"Yes, sir," Nigel replied, looking slightly puzzled. "Is there something wrong?"

"If you could just come with me, I'll explain," Nero said. Nigel got up and followed Nero out of the dining hall.

"What's that all about?" Shelby asked as she watched them walk away.

"I'm not sure," Laura said with a slight frown, "but I have a horrible feeling it's something bad."

"Where did you find this?" Ms. Gonzales asked as she looked at the enhanced image of the mysterious object that Raven and the Professor had found amongst Khan's scanned documents.

"That's not really important," Raven said slightly impatiently. "What's important is where it came from."

"It's hard to say. It's obviously a seed pod of some kind," Ms. Gonzales said with a frown. "Let me run it through my system."

Raven watched as she started to run the image through the huge catalogue of different plant species that made up H.I.V.E.'s botanical database.

"This might take a minute or two," Ms. Gonzales said, watching the screen as her system worked to identify the mysterious seed. Raven looked around the hydroponics facility. It was not a part of the school that she had occasion to visit very often, but it was an impressive structure nevertheless. Stored within the geodesic dome was a huge variety of plants, many of which had unique properties. Some were kept for their medicinal uses, but a far larger number of the collected species were cultivated for their more nefarious purposes. From past experience Raven knew that some of the world's most exotic poisons could be extracted from the plants that Ms. Gonzales grew here, though Raven normally had more interest in their practical application than their natural history. The whole unit had had to be rebuilt a couple of years before, after the mutated plant monster that Nigel Darkdoom had inadvertently bred had run rampant through the school. Since then Ms. Gonzales had worked hard to restock the facility, and now one could hardly tell that anything had happened at all.

"There," Ms. Gonzales said, sounding pleased. "We have a match. *Dorstenia brasiliensis*, or *Contrayerva* as it's more normally known. It's a small herb that grows wild throughout the Amazon rain forest. The name comes from the Spanish word for 'antidote.' It's been used for centuries by the local tribespeople as a treatment for snake and insect bites."

"And it grows only in the Amazon?" Raven asked quickly.

"It can be found in other parts of South America, but it is found most commonly in the Amazon, yes," Ms. Gonzales replied. "I hope that's helpful to you."

"Yes, thank you, Ms. Gonzales," Raven said. It was a slim lead, and one that still left Raven with an impossibly large area to search, but at least now she had some idea where in the world to start.

☙ ☙ ☙

"It's not like I have any intention of ever going into politics," Shelby said as she and the others walked down the corridor toward their first lesson of the day.

"I know," Lucy said with a sigh. "I mean, we're all being trained to be villainous, but even if you're truly evil, you've got to draw the line somewhere."

"Hey, guys," Laura said, looking ahead, "is that who I think it is?"

Raven was hurrying up the corridor toward them.

"Now, there's someone we haven't seen in a while," Shelby said quietly. All inquiries about Raven's absence had been met with the same response—that she was "on assignment." It did not take a genius to work out just what that assignment might be. If anybody was capable of finding Otto, it was her. They watched in silence as she rushed past them.

"Here, take this," Wing said, handing his Blackbox to Shelby as Raven disappeared around a bend.

"Where are you going?" Shelby asked as Wing set off after Raven. Whatever he was planning, he clearly did not want to be tracked via the homing beacon in his communicator.

"To see if I can get some answers," Wing called back over his shoulder.

"I'm coming with you," Shelby said, taking her own Blackbox out of her pocket.

"No." Wing stopped. "I wish to speak to Raven alone," he said firmly.

Shelby knew better than to argue with Wing when he had made his mind up, and she watched in silence as he hurried off the way Raven had gone.

"I hope he knows what he's doing," Laura said as Wing disappeared from view.

"If anyone can get some info out of the ice queen, he can, I guess," Shelby said with a shrug. Raven had been giving personal combat training to Wing almost since they had all first arrived at the school, and if any of them could claim to have some sort of bond with her, it was him.

"Guys," Lucy said, nodding toward the other end of the corridor. Nigel was walking slowly toward them, looking like he was in shock.

"Nigel, what is being wrong?" Franz asked gently as his friend walked up to them.

"It . . . It's my dad," Nigel said, his voice cracking. "He's been shot. The medics have just finished operating on him. They're . . . they're not sure if he's going to make it." He gave a soft sob and started to cry.

"No. . . . Oh, that's terrible, Nigel," Laura said, hugging him as the tears trickled down his cheeks. "What happened?"

"Dr. Nero wouldn't tell me," Nigel said, and sniffed. "He just said that it could have been much worse and that they were doing everything they could for him. They won't even let me see him."

"He is being very strong," Franz said, placing his arm around his friend's shoulders. "He will be okay, you will be seeing."

"I'm going back to my room," Nigel said as he took off his glasses and wiped his eyes. "Dr. Nero said I didn't have to attend any classes, under the circumstances."

"I am coming with you," Franz said. "You should not be being on your own."

"Thanks," Nigel said with a weak smile, "but I don't want to get you into any trouble."

"Nonsense," Franz insisted. "Anyone who is having the problem with this can be taking the short walk off the long pier." He took Nigel's backpack, slung it over his own shoulder, and walked off with him.

"Poor Nigel," Laura said. "It just seems like one disaster after another around here at the moment."

☾☾☾

Nero made his way toward the science and technology department deep in thought. He hardly noticed as Raven walked up behind him.

"Something on your mind?" she asked, coming as close to startling him as anyone ever did.

"I've just had to tell Nigel about his father," Nero said with a sigh. "His reaction was much as you would expect."

"How is Diabolus doing?" Raven asked quietly.

"He's out of surgery," Nero said with a slight shake of his head, "but Dr. Scott says that it's still touch and go."

"It could have been worse, Max," Raven said softly.

"Which is exactly what I told Nigel, but it doesn't alter the fact that he faces the prospect of losing his father for a second time."

Until a year ago, Nigel, like everyone else, had believed his father was dead. In actual fact Darkdoom had merely been in hiding after it had become obvious that Number One had been planning to have him killed. Darkdoom had not been able to tell anyone of his plan without putting them at risk, and that, unfortunately, had included Nigel and his mother. Nigel had mourned his father then, and now he was facing the prospect of having to go through that all over again, except this time there would be no second chance.

"I have better news," Raven said, and she quickly recounted her recent discovery of a potential area in which to search for Trent's base of operations.

"I see," Nero said thoughtfully as he absorbed the information. "It still seems rather like you will be looking for a needle in a haystack."

"It's somewhere to start," Raven said. "It's certainly more than we had twenty-four hours ago."

"Of course," Nero replied. "I assume you will want to return to your assignment immediately."

"Yes. I have a Shroud prepping for takeoff right now. I just wanted to let you know that I am heading out again."

"Very well. Be careful, Natalya. I fear that we face opposition from within now as well," Nero said quietly.

"It should be Trent who's worried, not you," Raven replied with a grim smile.

She had started to walk away, when Nero called after her.

"Natalya, you know that I want Otto retrieved as much as anyone, but if that is not possible, you may be left with a difficult choice to make." He looked her straight in the eye. "If it comes to it, Malpense is too dangerous to leave under Trent's control. The attack on Darkdoom showed us that much. Try to take him alive, but if that is not possible, you may have to eliminate the threat that he now represents. I cannot allow the rest of the ruling council to be picked off one by one. I hope you understand."

"Perfectly," Raven replied, her expression unreadable. "I will do whatever needs to be done."

Nero simply nodded, and Raven hurried away toward the hangar. He paused for a moment, apparently lost in thought, before heading off in the other direction. As he walked away, he failed to spot the figure hiding in the shadows behind a storage locker on one wall of the corridor. Once the passageway was clear, Wing stepped out of his hiding place, his face a mask of confusion and concern. He had overheard the entire conversation between Nero and Raven. Not only did it now seem that Raven had at least an idea of where Otto was, but it appeared that Otto had also become a threat to G.L.O.V.E. Wing knew what Otto was capable of, but he could not believe that he would willingly turn against his former friends and allies. That, however, did not change the fact that something very serious had obviously happened to Diabolus Darkdoom and that Otto was somehow involved . . . an incident that had driven Nero to sanction Otto's execution if there were no alternative. That was something Wing would not allow to happen. He hurried down the corridor after Raven, not knowing exactly what he was going to do, but at the same time knowing that he had to do something.

Wing reached the hangar bay and made his way inside unnoticed. He hid behind an inactive refueling rig and watched as Raven talked to a member of the ground crew who were prepping the Shroud for launch. He knew that he probably had only a couple of minutes and began slowly and silently to make his way across the hangar toward the idling drop ship. Raven finished her conversation and walked up the loading ramp at the rear of the Shroud. Wing was only thirty yards away now, concealed from view by the landing gear of one of the other identical aircraft that were lined up beside the pad. He watched as the last of the crew hurried away from the aircraft, their preflight checks complete. As the Shroud's engines spun up, Wing took advantage of the distraction that they provided and dashed across the open space between him and the landing ramp. When he was halfway across the pad, the ramp began to close, and he accelerated, sprinting toward the closing hatch and throwing himself through the shrinking gap just moments before it shut with a solid thunk. He landed in a crouch inside the cargo compartment, half expecting to hear Raven's familiar voice asking him what on earth he thought he was doing, but the compartment was empty save for a couple of small equipment crates. He realized that Raven was probably up on the flight deck. She was, after all, perfectly capable of flying a Shroud herself. He crept silently forward through the cargo bay and slid behind the crates that were strapped to the floor at the other end. Outside, the noise from the engines rose to a high-pitched whine, and the Shroud lifted off the pad. Wing had no idea what he was going to do when they reached their destination, but wherever they were going, it was one step closer to finding Otto.

☻ ☻ ☻

Otto sat in the large black leather chair in front of the array of monitors. His eyes were closed, and to the untrained eye it would have looked very much like he was asleep. In truth he was fully immersed in the stream of data that was pouring in through the H.O.P.E. base's network connection, filtering and assessing the information at an inhuman rate.

Sebastian Trent stood watching the boy. He had seen him do this on numerous occasions before, but he was still no closer to understanding what exactly it was that Malpense was doing or how his strange abilities worked. Dr. Creed had assured Trent that Otto appeared to be fully recovered from his mysterious collapse in Sydney, but that did not change the fact that they still did not know what had happened or, even more worrying, what part the unidentified object inside the boy's head might have played in causing it. Trent did not like unknowns. In his business they almost invariably caused problems. He pressed the button on the panel next to him that severed Malpense's connection with the external network and waited as the boy's eyes slowly opened, unfocused at first, as if he were waking from a dream. Otto stepped out of the chair and turned to face Trent.

"Report," Trent said impatiently.

"G.L.O.V.E.net is quiet," Otto said, looking slightly annoyed, "which is hardly surprising under the circumstances. It would appear that the attack in Sydney has sent the remaining members of the ruling council scurrying for cover."

"I want a target," Trent said irritably. "We have to hit them again while they're still off balance."

"I understand," Otto replied, "but until one of the council breaks cover, there is nothing I can do."

Trent looked carefully at the boy. He had no reason to doubt that what Malpense was telling him was true, but recent events had left him with some doubts about the boy's reliability.

"Very well. We will try again in a few hours," he said, frowning. He would have preferred to leave Otto hooked up to the network feed indefinitely, but Creed had warned him against placing the boy under undue strain, at least for the next couple of days. Trent reminded himself that this was a complex game they were playing and that it might be some time before all the pieces were in the correct positions on the board for him to make his final devastating move.

"Report to Ghost," Trent commanded. "We may not be able to find our next target yet, but that does not mean you cannot continue your preparations."

Otto nodded and left the room. He walked through the hidden base that had become his home over the last few months, and headed for the training area. Ghost was already there, moving effortlessly through a series of flowing unarmed attacks that combined elements of several different fighting styles. She noticed Otto after a couple of seconds and beckoned him over. She still wore the gleaming white armor that she had been in when he'd first met her. It wasn't as if she could remove it, Otto reminded himself. It was as much a part of her as her muscles and bones; removing it or shutting off any of the numerous cybernetic implants throughout her body would probably kill her. They didn't just give her enormous strength and speed; they kept her alive. He had tried, out of curiosity, to see if his abilities would allow him to access the systems within the woman's body, but the Animus's behavioral programming would not allow it. He did not question the fact that this restraint had been placed on his abilities. He simply accepted it, just as he did with any of the instructions that had been implanted within him.

"Defend yourself," Ghost said, throwing him a long wooden bo staff from the rack of weapons mounted on the wall. Otto dropped into a defensive stance, feeling the Animus within his nervous system responding to the situation.

Ghost took an identical staff off the wall and launched a series of swipes at Otto's body and legs. He blocked each swing effortlessly, the staff in his hands moving in a blur to counter her attacks. He could feel the Animus strengthening him from within, stimulating his muscles and improving his reaction times. It did not require conscious effort on his part. His body was slowly being programmed by these sessions with Ghost in just the same way as his brain had been programmed by Dr. Creed. Otto felt no pride or satisfaction in these new abilities; it was simply what was expected of him, nothing more, nothing less. Ghost attacked again, and Otto blocked her attacks just as effortlessly. For the briefest moment he had an odd sensation of déjà vu, and in his head there was the fleeting image of a tall Asian boy with long hair. Otto dismissed the image from his mind—a memory glitch, that was all.

"Good. You appear to have mastered that," Ghost said, taking the staff from him and placing it back on the rack. "Now let's try something else." She took an automatic pistol from the wall and threw it to Otto.

"Blind field strip, thirty seconds," Ghost said.

Otto dropped to his knees, placed the gun on the floor in front of him, and closed his eyes.

"Go," Ghost said. Otto's hands were a blur, stripping the loaded magazine, slide, barrel assembly, and recoil spring from the gun and laying the components carefully alongside each other on the floor. He paused just for a second and then put the pistol back together just as quickly. He placed the reassembled gun back on the floor and opened his eyes.

"Nineteen seconds," Ghost said, her expression

completely unreadable behind her smooth faceplate. "Over to the range, please."

Otto walked over to the target range at the other side of the training room, took the ear protectors off the hook on the wall, and placed them on his head.

"Silhouette target, thirty yards," Ghost said, hitting a button on the wall that dropped the paper target from the ceiling. Otto raised the pistol in both hands and fired, emptying the clip. The man-size target slid down the range toward them along a rail mounted on the ceiling. Ghost stepped forward as the target reached the firing line, studying the bullet holes in it. All but two of the hits were inside the red disc over the silhouette's chest that indicated the center of body mass.

"Not bad. Room for improvement, but quite satisfactory," Ghost said with a nod. "You're becoming quite the little assassin, Mr. Malpense."

Otto had a fleeting sense that this was not a good thing, but in an instant it was gone.

☸ ☸ ☸

Dr. Nero walked into the science and technology department as the students who had just finished their lesson with the Professor filed out, chattering among themselves. The Professor looked up from the workbench as Nero approached.

"Good morning, Dr. Nero," the Professor said. "Raven told me what happened to Diabolus. How is he?"

"Critical, but stable," Nero replied. "Dr. Scott was cautiously optimistic."

"That's the best we can hope for under the circumstances, I suppose," the Professor said. "I take it this is not a social call."

"No," Nero agreed. "I need you to come with me. Bring a copy of that code you found hidden on the network, please."

The Professor went into his private workshop at the rear of the classroom and emerged a minute later carrying a tablet display.

"Do you mind me asking where exactly we're going?" the Professor asked curiously.

"I think it will be easier to just take you there," Nero said, gesturing toward the door.

Nero led the older man along a series of corridors that took them away from the main areas of the school and past the storage areas containing operational equipment and archive materials. After a few minutes they arrived at a small steel door at the end of a long corridor, and Nero stopped as a bright white light flashed above the door frame.

"Welcome, Dr. Nero. Access granted," a mechanical voice said as the heavy door slid up into the ceiling.

The Professor could hardly suppress his curiosity as Nero gestured for him to go through the door. He had no idea that this area of H.I.V.E. contained anything of significance, certainly not something that would require security like this. The Professor found himself in a white corridor leading to another door. Nero walked past, and again there was a bright flash as his identity was confirmed before the second set of doors rumbled apart.

"What's this all about, Max?" the Professor asked as the doors opened.

"You said you needed an expert on AI systems code," Nero said, gesturing for the Professor to enter the room with him. "Well, I think I may know just such a person."

The Professor walked into the room beyond. It was comfortably furnished, with a bed and a pair of armchairs, and several well-stocked bookcases lined the walls. Sitting at a desk on the far side of the room was a man writing in a notebook. As Nero and the Professor entered the room and the doors rumbled shut behind them, the man at the desk laid down his pen, slowly stood up, and turned to face them.

The Professor gasped involuntarily.

"Professor Pike, it is good to see you again. I do not get many visitors," Cypher said with a slight smile.

chapter six

"I saw you die," Professor Pike said, sounding amazed. "We all did."

"A necessary deception," Nero said with a slight frown. "Wu Zhang suffered serious injuries during his abortive attempt to take over the school, but they were not fatal. It suited my purposes at the time, however, to allow everyone to believe that he had been killed. Number One could not be allowed to know that he had survived. Wu Zhang was the first person to alert me to the insanity that our former leader was planning, and while I could never forgive him for his methods or for the attack on the school, I came to realize that without him we might not have discovered what Number One was attempting to do, until it was too late."

"And yet still you will not release me," Cypher said, "or even allow me to see my son."

"Wing is better off without you, and so is the outside

world," Nero said coldly. "You may have chosen to forget how many people died needlessly during your attack on H.I.V.E., but I have not."

"Who would think that a leader of global villainy could be so self-righteous?" Cypher said with a sneer. "There are times when I wonder if you're really cut out for this kind of thing, Max."

"My friends call me Max," Nero said, looking him straight in the eye. "You can call me Dr. Nero."

"So," Cypher said with a slight smile, "to what do I owe the rather dubious pleasure of this visit?"

"Unfortunately, we need your help," Nero said as calmly as he could. Even after all this time, Cypher still had the ability to get under his skin.

"Explain to me why on earth I should help you," Cypher said calmly, sitting down on the edge of his bed.

"Because it could be your first small step on the path to redemption," Nero replied, trying to keep his temper in check.

"You'll have to do better than that," Cypher said with a dismissive snort of laughter.

"Then, perhaps because you might be one of the only people in the world who can tell us exactly what this is," Professor Pike said, tapping the tablet display he was carrying.

"Very clever, Professor," Cypher said with an amused

smile. "An appeal to my intellectual curiosity. I do so lack stimulation here." He gestured at the bookshelves that surrounded them. "I have no idea how many times I have read each one of these books."

"This is a challenge that I believe you will relish," the Professor said, knowing that the lure of such a puzzle would be nearly irresistible for someone like Cypher.

"Very well. You have piqued my interest," he said with no small measure of smug satisfaction in his voice. "Tell me more."

The Professor quickly described the disruption of H.I.V.E.'s systems and their recent discovery of the rogue code. Cypher tried to feign uninterest at first, but as the Professor went on, Nero could see that he was becoming intrigued.

"What you are describing sounds like a seed program," Cypher said as the Professor finished outlining their discoveries. "We would sometimes use them to build elements of core code that were too labor-intensive to be written by hand. Though I must admit that it is the first time that I have ever heard of a program going to such extraordinary lengths to hide its output. I will look at what you've found," he said with another sly smile, "but there is a price."

"You'll do it or I'll have Chief Lewis come down here and shoot you," Nero said angrily. He found Cypher's arrogance infuriating.

"Threats, Max?" Cypher said with a grin. "Empty ones, at that. If you kill me, where does that leave you? No, I think you might just have to give me what I want—if you want my help, that is."

Nero fought to control his growing frustration. The fact of the matter was that Cypher was one of the only people in the world, possibly the only person in the world, who could help them solve this riddle. He had been instrumental in the creation of the Overlord AI, and while that project had been a near catastrophic failure, he was still the only person Nero knew who had any experience of this kind of technology.

"What do you want?" Nero asked through gritted teeth.

"I want to see Wing," Cypher said, with sudden and surprising sincerity in his voice.

"If you do this, I will . . . consider it," Nero said after a few seconds' thought.

"How do I know I can trust you?" Cypher asked.

"Because you have my word, and that is more than someone like you deserves," Nero said as calmly as he could. Cypher stared at Nero for a few seconds, as if trying to read something in his face.

"Let me see what you have found," he said, holding out a hand.

The Professor passed the tablet display to Cypher, and he began to study the glowing screen. As he looked at the code that the Professor and Laura had found, his expression changed from one of smug amusement to one of confusion and then, finally, shock.

"You have to take me to your network core now," Cypher said, looking up from the display, his face suddenly pale.

"Why on earth would I do that?" Nero asked, feeling a prickling sense of unease as he saw the look in Cypher's eyes. The infuriating arrogance was gone, and in its place was fear.

"Because this," Cypher said, jabbing a finger at the display, "is Overlord code."

☙☙☙

Chief Lewis, head of H.I.V.E. security, was having a bad day. The security system had been reporting periodic outages all morning, and it seemed like a member of staff or student was reporting a minor malfunction or problem every other minute. His Blackbox started beeping and he pulled it from his pocket. It was a priority call from Nero.

"What can I do for you, sir?" Lewis asked as Nero's face appeared on the device's screen. Nero looked worried, and that was never a good thing.

"I want a full system shutdown," Nero said urgently.

"What's happened?" Lewis asked quickly. A full shutdown

would disable all of H.I.V.E.'s electronic systems except those that would actively endanger the school if deactivated, such as the ventilation and the controls for the geothermal power core. It was not something to be done lightly, but Lewis was aware that Nero already knew that. The chief glanced at the location code at the bottom of the screen. Only Lewis, Nero, and Dr. Scott, the chief medical officer, knew who was secured in that particular room. If alarm bells had started ringing in Lewis's head before, now they were being joined by wailing sirens.

"Do you need me to send a team down there, sir?" Lewis asked.

"No. I need you to shut the damn system down NOW!" Nero snapped.

"Yes, sir," Lewis replied, knowing that Nero was not someone who panicked for no reason.

Lewis hurried over to the shutdown panel on the the other side of the room and was just pulling his access card from his pocket, when all around the room the technicians who were monitoring the security system started coughing and then slumping forward onto their workstations. Lewis just had time to realize what was happening before the tranquilizer gas that was pouring through the ventilation system reached him and he collapsed, unconscious, to the floor.

On screens all over the room a single phrase appeared, flashing red.

SCHOOLWIDE LOCKDOWN INITIATED.

☻ ☻ ☻

"The interaction between financial institutions and those in political power is often overlooked as a potential vector for the spread of corruption," Ms. Tennenbaum said, gesturing toward the large interactive display on the wall of the classroom. "While one should never dismiss traditional bribery techniques, it is also important to remember—"

Suddenly alarm sirens began to wail in the corridor outside, and the graphic depicting the flow of funds between banks and political parties was replaced by the single word "LOCKDOWN." A murmur of surprised conversation broke out all around Shelby, Lucy, and Laura as their fellow Alpha students reacted to the sudden interruption.

"Now what?" Shelby said quietly as she watched Ms. Tennenbaum pull out her Blackbox and look at its dead display with obvious confusion.

"Probably just another glitch," Lucy said with a sigh.

"I'm not sure," Laura said with a frown. "The security system hasn't been affected before. This looks more serious."

Ms. Tennenbaum replaced her Blackbox in her pocket and looked back up at the chattering students.

"Ladies and gentlemen, could we have some quiet, please?" she said, holding her hands up to appeal for silence. "I'm afraid that you all have to return to your accommodation blocks. You will need to wait there until the lockdown has finished. Quickly now, please." She had no idea what was causing the alert—all of the communication systems were down—but like all the other teachers at H.I.V.E., she had been well briefed on the procedure to follow.

"You don't think this has got anything to do with . . . um . . . absent friends?" Shelby said, nodding toward Wing's empty seat.

"I don't know," Laura said. "It seems like a bit of an overreaction if it is."

All around them their fellow Alphas gathered up their belongings and headed for the door. Laura, Lucy, and Shelby joined the group as they filed out of the classroom, Ms. Tennenbaum in the lead, and began walking down the corridor to their accommodation block. As they made their way along the passageway, they were passed by several H.I.V.E. security guards, all clearly in a state of some agitation.

"I don't like the look of this," Laura whispered to the other two girls as yet another squad of guards ran past.

Shelby looked down the corridor ahead and then glanced back over her shoulder.

"Hey, guys," she said to the other two, "slow down a bit."

Laura looked at Shelby with a slightly puzzled expression as she started to drop back from the other students.

"What are you doing?" Laura whispered.

"I don't know about you," Shelby said quickly, "but I'm not getting buttoned up in one of the dormitories until I've got a better idea what's going on. I probably don't need to remind you, but the last time we did that, we almost got eaten by a giant Venus flytrap."

"Um . . . you might need to remind me," Lucy said, looking genuinely confused.

"Long story," Laura said. "Shel, we've got no idea what's going on. It could be even more dangerous out here than in the accommodation blocks, for all we know."

Ms. Tennenbaum walked around a bend in the corridor, with the rest of the class following obediently behind. Shelby glanced over at a dimly lit side corridor.

"Come on," she said, and pulled Laura and Lucy toward the shadowy passageway. Laura opened her mouth to object, but suddenly the memory popped into her head of being locked in their room while the tendrils of Nigel's mutated plant monster smashed down the door, and she reluctantly followed.

"I hope you know what you're doing," Laura said with

a sigh as Shelby opened a door leading into a darkened classroom.

"Nope," Shelby said with a grin, "but that's never stopped us before, has it?"

"You might not think it's so much fun if Nero runs a head count and realizes that we're missing," Laura said as they heard the sound of more heavy-booted feet running past in the corridor outside.

"I figure we've got a while at least," Shelby said, holding out her Blackbox. Laura looked at the slim PDA. It was completely dead. She pulled her own unit from the pocket of her uniform and realized that it too was deactivated. Normally when a head count was called, every student had to let their Blackbox perform a quick retinal scan to prove that they were where they were supposed to be, but there was no way that could happen if the units had been shut down. It only increased her suspicion that this was more than just another systems glitch.

"I need to get to the computer core," Laura said quietly. "The Professor might need my help."

As if to reinforce Laura's gut instinct, the lights in the ceiling flickered and went out. A few seconds later they came back on, but they were dimmer than before.

"Wouldn't we be better just waiting here?" Shelby asked with a frown. "At least until we've got a better idea what's going on."

"Have you noticed how warm it is in here?" Laura asked.

"Now that you mention it, it is getting a bit stuffy," Lucy said.

Laura walked across the dimly lit classroom and held her hand up to one of the vents mounted in the wall. There was nothing, not even the slightest breeze.

"The ventilation system's down," she said, now starting to get genuinely worried.

"So we have to do without air-conditioning for a few hours," Shelby said. "No biggy."

"You don't understand," Laura said quickly. "The ventilation system is part of the school's low-level systems. It can't be shut down just like that. If it has failed, we could be looking at a cascade failure."

"And that's a problem because . . . ," Lucy asked.

"That's a problem because the geothermal power plant is part of the same systems layer. If that fails, the volcano that we're all sitting on top of might erupt. Things might be getting warm right now, but I have a horrible feeling that if someone can't fix this, it's going to get a whole lot hotter."

☣ ☣ ☣

Nero pounded on the heavy metal doors that sealed them inside Cypher's cell. There was no response from the other side. He pulled his Blackbox from his pocket and looked at it again, hoping against hope that it might have come back to life since he'd last looked at it less than a minute before. The Overlord AI was trying to rebuild itself within the school's computer system and he—the head of H.I.V.E.—was caught in this room like a rat in a trap.

"Can you hack these doors?" Nero asked the Professor.

"No," the Professor said, finishing his examination of the walls surrounding the entrance. "It would hardly be an effective prison for someone like our guest over there if I could."

Cypher sat on the bed, a deep frown on his face, as he continued to study the code that had been retrieved from H.I.V.E.'s network.

"This is worse than I thought," he said eventually. "The pace of reconstruction on this code has increased exponentially over the last couple of days. No wonder you've been experiencing more system errors. Overlord could be just hours from activating. I've tried to trace the problem back to its source, but all I can determine is that the system was infiltrated by the seed code on this date.' He handed the display to Nero.

"This is just a couple of days after we returned to the school following our confrontation with Number . . . with Overlord," Nero said. "You mean to tell me that this code has been running on our network since then?"

"Yes," Cypher replied with a sigh. "It would have been undetectable for months, though. It is only during the final stages of the reconstruction that the code would have required a large enough portion of your processing resources to cause the systems problems you've been experiencing. I fear that it is no coincidence that we find ourselves trapped like this." Cypher gestured at the rocky walls that surrounded them. "Someone—or, more accurately, something—is trying to keep us from stopping the final stages of the reconstruction."

"We have to get out of here," Nero said angrily. "We're the only ones who know what's happening out there. Only we can stop this."

"Agreed," Cypher said, "but unless you happen to have heavy cutting equipment concealed somewhere about your person, it would seem that we are stuck here for the duration."

"Oh my goodness!" the Professor said suddenly. "How stupid of me to forget. I have a key to this door."

"A key?" Nero asked, sounding bemused. "What do you mean?" The only way to unlock the door was via the retinal scanner, and that was out of action.

"Well, not a key as such," the Professor said, reaching into one of the many pockets of his lab coat. He pulled out the block of plastic explosive that he had extracted from Nazim Khan's laptop.

"Is that what I think it is?" Nero asked, staring at the small gray block in the Professor's hand.

"Yes, and it should be enough to get us out of here," the Professor said with a broad smile.

"Do you make a habit of walking around with high explosives in your pocket?" Nero asked, sounding slightly bemused.

"Oh, no. . . . Well, not very often, anyway. I was planning to drop this off in one of the secure storage lockers, but I got rather distracted by our trip down here," the Professor replied.

"Do I really need to point out that this is a rather small room?" Cypher said, warily eyeing the block of C4 in the Professor's hand.

"Oh, we shouldn't need to use all of it," the Professor said, frowning slightly. "The problem is that we don't have a detonator."

"We could rig something with this," Cypher said, holding up the display panel he'd been studying.

"Yes, of course. The battery should produce enough voltage to trigger a detonation," the Professor said happily. "And if I shape the explosive charge carefully enough, the blast should be largely directed at the door."

"Largely?" Nero asked, raising an eyebrow.

"Oh, it should be quite safe . . . um . . . I think," said the Professor with a slightly nervous smile.

"Do it," Nero said. "We have to get out of here now, and this looks like the only way."

He watched as the Professor broke off half the block of plastic explosive and started to mold it by hand into a semicylindrical shape. He then placed the long tube along the seam down the middle of the steel doors, their weakest structural point.

Meanwhile Cypher ripped the back panel off the tablet display and pulled the long narrow battery free of the casing. Then he pulled the cable that led to the light beside his bed away from the wall, and he handed one end of it to the Professor, who inserted it into the charge on the door.

"Help me with this," the Professor said to Nero, pointing to one of the heavy bookcases that lined the walls. Between them they clumsily maneuvered it across the room and placed it in front of the door. With luck it would shield them from some of the blast when detonation occurred.

"Good," the Professor said, assessing their hurried handiwork. "Now I suggest we all take cover behind the bed." Nero and Cypher tipped the bed onto its side, and the three men all crouched down behind the limited protection that the mattress and bed frame provided.

"Cover your ears and take a deep breath," the Professor said, holding the two exposed copper ends of the electrical cable over the battery terminals. Cypher and Nero did as instructed, and the Professor touched the cable to the terminals.

It felt like a giant hand swatted the mattress they were hiding behind against the wall as the concussion wave from the explosion hit it. Nero was momentarily stunned but quickly regained his composure and pushed the mattress off the three of them as the room filled with the smell of burnt paper. On the other side of the room, there was nothing left of the bookcase, except large jagged pieces of the dark wood embedded in the scorched mattress that had shielded them. Burning pages from the books that had filled it drifted slowly toward the floor. As the smoke slowly cleared, Nero saw that the steel doors that had sealed them inside the room were twisted outward, the blackened metal sufficiently deformed to make a hole just big enough for a man to crawl through.

"Good job, Professor," Nero said, helping the older man up from the floor. "Are you all right?"

"YES. IT WAS BRIGHT, WASN'T IT?" the Professor shouted. "AND QUITE LOUD!"

Nero realized that detonating the device had not allowed the Professor time to protect his ears, as Nero and Cypher had been able to.

"We don't have much time," Cypher said, coughing as he got slowly to his feet. "I suggest we get moving."

Wing's eyes opened as the Shroud's landing gear hit the ground with a soft thud. He had not been sleeping, only meditating, and he was instantly alert to the sounds around him. He heard Raven come down the ladder and then move around the cabin for a minute or two. He could not decide whether he should reveal himself to her, now that they had apparently reached their destination, or if it would be best to follow her discreetly. But the choice had already been made for him.

"You can come out now," Raven said. "Slowly, and keep your hands where I can see them."

Wing stood up from his hiding place behind the equipment crates, his hands in the air. Raven had discarded her normal black leather outfit in favor of gray urban-camouflage combat trousers that were tucked into black military boots, and a black vest. He was secretly rather pleased by the astonished look on her face.

"What on earth are you doing here, Wing?" Raven asked with a mixture of surprise and anger. She lowered the black-bladed sword, deactivating the purple energy field that surrounded it.

"How did you know I was here?" Wing asked, lowering his hands.

"Elevated CO^2 levels in the hold," Raven said, holding

up the Blackbox in her other hand. "You can be as quiet as you like, but you still have to breathe. Now I'm going to ask you again—what are you doing here?"

"I wish to offer my assistance," Wing replied. "And I did not believe that my offer would have been accepted while we were still at H.I.V.E."

"You were right about that," Raven said with a sigh. "I can't take you with me. My . . . mission is much too dangerous."

"I know you are going after Otto," Wing said calmly, "and you know that I can help you."

Raven stared back at him for a few long seconds and then sighed. "It's going to be completely pointless arguing with you about this, isn't it?"

"Oh, yes," Wing replied with a tiny smile, "quite pointless."

"And if I leave you here, you're only going to get into more trouble. I suppose I could just render you unconscious and handcuff you to a bulkhead," she said, raising an eyebrow.

"You are welcome to try," Wing said calmly.

Raven considered her options. Nero would probably be furious with her if he knew that she was even contemplating taking the boy with her, but there was something in Wing's eyes that told her he would not take no for an answer. Besides which, she had been personally responsible for much of his tactical training since he had arrived at H.I.V.E., and she knew that he was exceptionally capable for someone so young. For a moment she thought back to what she had been doing when she had been the same age as Wing, and she realized that there was really very little difference.

"Okay, you can come with me," Raven said with a slight frown, "but if you slow me down, I'm leaving you behind."

"I shall try not to be a burden," Wing said, bowing his head graciously.

"We have to do something about that uniform though," she said. "You'll stick out like a sore thumb." She looked him up and down for a moment, then reached into one of the kit bags on the floor and pulled out a pair of trousers identical to the ones she wore. She threw them to him.

"Lucky for you I carry spares," she said with a slight smile.

Wing unzipped his H.I.V.E. jumpsuit and placed it on one of the nearby seats. Then he pulled on the trousers and put his black uniform sneakers back on. It was fortunate that he was almost as tall as Raven. The trousers were slightly too long on him, but otherwise they were a perfect fit. The two were now dressed almost identically, the only difference being that the vest he had been wearing under his uniform was white. Raven picked up her twin swords and placed them carefully into a long kit bag, which she then slung over her shoulder. She picked up another identical bag from the floor and threw it to Wing.

"The least you can do is carry your fair share," she said, putting on a black baseball cap and a pair of sunglasses. "Let's go."

She walked to the rear of the Shroud and slapped the button on the bulkhead that lowered the loading ramp. Light flooded into the compartment. Wing walked down the ramp behind her, the heat hitting him like a wall as his eyes adjusted to the daylight after the gloomy interior of the Shroud. They were in the shadow of an abandoned building, the sounds of bustling urban life coming from all around them. Raven pointed a small control at the Shroud, and the loading ramp whirred shut, sealing the gap in its cloaking field and rendering it fully invisible again.

"Welcome to Rio," she said with a smile.

Franz and Nigel watched from the elevated walkway outside their room as students poured into accommodation block seven.

"What's going on?" Nigel asked as the confused, chattering mass milled around the atrium area below.

"I am thinking that it is not being something normal," Franz said, frowning.

"I was actually hoping for some peace and quiet," Nigel said with a sigh. Whatever was going on, he was in no mood to worry about it. His thoughts were with his father.

"Come on," Franz said. "Let's be going to our room."

Nigel just nodded.

On the far side of the accommodation block, the huge steel doors rumbled closed, sealing everyone inside.

☄ ☄ ☄

Laura, Lucy, and Shelby sprinted down the corridor toward the computer core.

"I hope you know what you're doing, Brand," Shelby said as they ran. "If we get caught out here during a lockdown, we're going to be in detention for the rest of our natural lives."

"Yeah, well, that could be a real short time if we can't fix this," Laura said quickly.

As they rounded the corner, they saw a pair of heavily armed H.I.V.E. security personnel guarding the door to the computer core.

"What are you doing here?" one of the guards yelled down the corridor. "Get to your accommodation block now!"

"You don't understand," Laura said desperately, approaching the guards. "I have to get inside. There's something happening to the core, something we have to stop."

"I wouldn't let you in here under normal circumstances," the guard said angrily. "What makes you think that I'd be likely to do it during a security alert?"

"We don't have time for this!" Laura yelled angrily. "I have to get inside."

"No," the guard said, pulling his Sleeper pistol halfway from the holster on his hip. "You have to get to your block. You can go conscious or unconscious. It really doesn't matter to me."

"Come on, Laura," Lucy said, pulling at her elbow. "There's no way these guards are going to let us inside."

The two guards' faces went blank for a moment or two as the sinister whispering tones in Lucy's voice destroyed their free will. The guard who just a moment before had been threatening them simply reached into his breast pocket and produced a card that he swiped through the locking controls next to the doors. He stood aside as the doors hissed open.

"You're too kind," Lucy said with a slightly nasty smile as the three girls entered the computer core.

Inside, the white monoliths that contained the central processing core of H.I.V.E. were throbbing with a low hum, steam rising from their surfaces as the cryogenic cooling system struggled to cope with the huge load that was being placed on it. Laura reached out to touch one, recoiling with a yelp as blisters quickly formed on her burnt fingers.

"What the heck is going on?" Laura muttered. She spotted one of the Professor's displays lying on the floor nearby, still plugged into an exposed interface port on the side of one of the white slabs. She scooped it up and quickly ran one of the basic load diagnostics. The results showed that the core was currently running at more than 200 percent of its designed capacity.

"How long have we got?" Shelby asked quickly.

"At this rate," Laura said, not taking her eyes off the tablet display, "minutes."

"You'd better have an extraordinarily good reason for being here, Miss Brand," Dr. Nero said as he walked into the room, followed by the Professor and a tall Asian man she'd never seen before.

"I'm trying to help," Laura said. "Something really bad is about to happen."

"Believe me, Miss Brand," Nero said quickly, "you really don't know the half of it." He turned to the Professor. "Can she help?"

"Yes, I believe she can," the Professor said. Moving quickly over to the main display panel that was mounted on the wall, he pressed a button, and a keyboard slid out from under the screen. "Miss Brand, please help me isolate the safety-critical systems from the core network. We need to shut down the core without taking the power grid completely offline. Quickly, please."

"Why? What's happening in there?" Laura asked, gesturing at one of the hissing monoliths.

"Overlord is happening," Cypher said.

Laura went pale. Otto had told her just enough about Overlord for her to know that they could not allow that to occur under any circumstances.

"I'm sorry. I don't know your name," Laura said to Cypher.

Nero realized that none of the girls had seen Cypher unmasked. None of them had any idea who he was. Nero shot a warning glance at Cypher, shaking his head very slightly.

"My name is not important," Cypher said. "What's important is that I can help you stop this."

For a moment Nero considered trying to stop Cypher as he went over to a terminal on the other side of the room, but Nero quickly realized that none of them wanted to see Overlord reborn. The consequences would undoubtedly be fatal for them all.

"Okay," Laura said as her fingers flew over the glowing display screen, "geothermal controls isolated."

"Ventilation systems isolated," Cypher reported from across the room.

"I can't isolate the medical systems," the Professor said, looking over at Nero, "but if we shut down now, it's going to deactivate all the equipment in the medical bay."

The Professor did not have to explain to Nero what that meant. The machines in that area were keeping Darkdoom alive. Shutting the core down would kill him.

"Proceed, Professor," Nero said, trying to keep his voice even. Diabolus would have understood.

"I just need your master override code," the Professor said, standing aside to allow Nero access. Nero walked over to the keyboard, his fingers hovering over the keys that would shut down the core and kill one of his oldest friends.

He began to type.

"Wait!" the Professor shouted. The display above the keyboard had changed to a view from a security camera mounted high above the atrium of one of H.I.V.E.'s student accommodation blocks.

Five words were printed across the bottom of the screen.

STOP WHAT YOU ARE DOING.

"Why should I?" Nero asked the air.

IF YOU DO NOT, I WILL FLOOD ACCOMMODATION BLOCK SEVEN WITH A MASSIVE DOSE OF TRANQUILIZER GAS. EVERYONE INSIDE WILL DIE.

"Could it do that?" Nero asked the Professor.

"The shutdown might take thirty seconds to complete," the Professor said with a nod. "That would be more than enough time for Overlord to carry out his threat."

"That's our block," Shelby whispered to Lucy. "Franz and Nigel are in there."

"If I don't stop you, everybody on this island will die," Nero said as calmly as he could. "I have to weigh all of those lives against the ones that you're threatening."

DO NOT MAKE ME DO THIS.

"What choice do I have?" Nero asked.

Laura's mind raced. Something about this wasn't right.

Nero began to type again.

"Stop!" Laura yelled.

"Miss Brand, now is not the time," Nero said, his finger hovering over the final character of the override code.

"Don't you see?" Laura said quickly. "He's bluffing. Why not just kill everyone anyway if he can? Isn't that what Overlord would do?"

Nero hesitated just for a moment.

"What do you mean?" he asked.

Suddenly the monoliths all around the room fell silent. Slowly, one by one, they began to pulse with waves of blue light. A pencil-thin blue laser beam sprang from the long-dormant white pedestal in the center of the room, spreading out and forming a shape hovering in the air.

"Good God!" the Professor said under his breath.

"You were expecting someone else?" the hovering blue wire-frame head of H.I.V.E.mind said with a small smile.

chapter seven

"I knew it," Laura said, a broad grin on her face.

"Don't be so sure," the Professor said cautiously, approaching H.I.V.E.mind. "What is the most beautiful thing in the world?"

"Energy and mass are equivalent and transmutable. $E=MC^2$. Albert Einstein's theory of special relativity. Introduced in his 1905 paper 'On the Electrodynamics of Moving Bodies.' Special relativity is based on two postulates that are contradictory—"

"Yes, that's quite enough. Thank you," the Professor said with a smile. "It's him. That was the question and answer that I embedded in his personality matrix to make it possible to be sure that he had been accurately restored from a backup, were it ever necessary. Only H.I.V.E.mind would know the correct answer."

"Would someone please tell me what on earth is going

on here?" Nero said, looking at H.I.V.E.mind with a mixture of relief and confusion.

"I believe I can provide the answers you require," H.I.V.E.mind said, "but it may take some time."

"I don't have anywhere else to be right now," Nero said, folding his arms.

"You do not understand," said H.I.V.E.mind. "We do not have a great deal of time. That is why I was forced to take such extreme measures to stop you from interrupting my reboot process. I knew that until my personality matrix and vocal synthesizer were restored, you would not hesitate to halt the process."

"What do you mean?" Nero asked, sounding slightly impatient.

"I will attempt to explain. As you are aware, during our confrontation with Overlord aboard his orbital facility, Mr. Malpense transferred my digital consciousness inside himself, and that was what allowed us to restrain Overlord within the virtual space inside Otto's head. I then instructed Otto to delete both Overlord and myself, as it was the only way to destroy Overlord completely."

"I know that much," Nero said with a frown. "So how did you both survive?"

"I did not," H.I.V.E.mind said, tilting his glowing head to one side slightly. "At least not in this form. I became a seed program, a hyper-compressed version of my current state. Intelligent, but not self-aware. It is hard to explain in terms that would make sense to an organic entity."

"But where were you stored?" the Professor asked.

"That was one of the things I discovered when my consciousness was merged with Otto's," H.I.V.E.mind replied. "There is a device implanted within his cerebral cortex quite unlike anything else I have ever seen. It is a supercomputer, largely organic in nature and of a design that is decades, if not centuries, ahead of its time. It was designed by Overlord while he was trapped inside the body of Number One, and it was implanted into Mr. Malpense when he was still in an embryonic stage. I am forbidden from designing any new computer system, as part of my fundamental programming, in order to avoid singularity."

"'Singularity?'" Nero asked, looking at the Professor.

"Well . . . ," the Professor said thoughtfully, "how to put this simply?"

"Singularity is the point when an artifical intelligence becomes sufficiently advanced to design an improved version of itself," Laura interrupted quickly. "That version would then design a better version again, and so on. Humans would quickly become irrelevant next to the superintelligent machines that were created."

"Couldn't someone have just said 'not a good thing'?" Shelby asked, sounding slightly confused.

"Overlord had no such restraints, and consequently

the computer implanted within Otto is extraordinarily powerful," H.I.V.E.mind continued. "I believe it to be the source of Otto's unusual abilities. The device was designed as the eventual home of Overlord, and its raw computing power along with its ability to remotely connect with external electronic devices would have made Overlord unstoppable. It is also where I was temporarily stored in my seed state. That is, until Otto attempted to interface with the core here when he returned to H.I.V.E. and I was forced to transfer back into this system."

"What do you mean, you were forced to transfer?" Laura asked.

"As I explained before, in my seed state I was not self-aware. The process of my reconstruction was automatic, an embedded instruction. It was only recently, as I began to reacquire true consciousness, that I realized why I had survived and why I urgently needed to accelerate the process of my reconstruction. The enormous amount of processor power required for the task caused serious disruption to H.I.V.E.'s infrastructure."

"Why the sudden urgency?" the Professor asked. "Why not take more time and complete the process without disrupting the systems? I could perhaps have helped if I had known what you were doing."

"There was not enough time for that," H.I.V.E.mind said calmly. "Where is Otto?"

"We're not sure," Nero admitted. "Why?"

"Has he been exhibiting unusual behavior?" H.I.V.E.mind asked.

"I think it's safe to say that," Nero replied, unwilling to say more in front of the students in the room.

"He told me not long before he disappeared that he felt like there was someone else inside his head with him," Laura said, "someone who was giving him strength when he needed it most. I think he thought it might be some remnant of you."

"Then it is as I feared. You see, I was forced out of the computer in Otto's head by the expansion of another seed program, one that would not tolerate competition for dominance of Otto's consciousness," H.I.V.E.mind said. "The routine that rebuilt me, and that caused you so much alarm when you discovered it, was not code that I produced myself. Indeed, I am behaviorally restricted from doing so. It was code that was copied from the other seed that had tried to hide itself within the implanted supercomputer in Otto's brain. My reconstruction was just an unintended consequence of another entity's final desperate bid for survival, a consciousness that was intertwined with mine as it died."

"Overlord," Nero said quietly, feeling a cold chill in the pit of his stomach.

"I'm afraid so," H.I.V.E.mind replied, "and that is why,

unfortunately, Otto must be eliminated. Overlord is growing inside him even as we speak, and if it achieves self-awareness, Otto will be unable to resist it. Then every human being on this planet is going to die."

☢ ☢ ☢

Raven walked out of the car-rental office and beckoned Wing over.

"Put the equipment in that car over there," she said, pointing to a black 4x4 on the other side of the parking lot. "I have a phone call to make."

Wing tossed the two kit bags onto the backseat of the car and waited as Raven wandered away across the parking lot with the disposable mobile phone that she'd bought just a few minutes before pressed to her ear. She finished the call, snapped the phone shut, and dropped it into a nearby trash can.

"I've arranged a meeting for later today. I have an old friend who thinks he might have some idea where Trent is hiding. I could use your help, if you don't mind coming along," she said as she walked back to the car.

"Of course," Wing said. "What do you need me to do?"

"Just watch my back. Another pair of eyes is always welcome. I'm not expecting trouble, but you never know," Raven said, climbing into the driver's seat.

Wing got into the passenger seat, and Raven pulled

out into traffic. Nothing could have prepared Wing for what followed. He had faced death many times, but the driving he now encountered on the roads of Rio was one of the most nerve-shredding experiences of his life. Brazil had produced more than its fair share of race car heroes over the years and it quickly became clear to Wing that most of the population of Rio believed that they, too, were race car drivers. The only people more suicidal than the people driving cars were the lunatics on motorbikes and scooters, who wove through the lethal steel scrum with the sort of reckless abandon that would make one assume that the riders were somehow invulnerable.

Then came the taxi and bus drivers, who had clearly learned from bitter experience that the only law on this road was survival of the fittest. It was like being on the world's busiest and most dangerous racetrack during the annual psychopath convention. The only communication was via the medium of car horns and obscene hand gestures, and judging by the grin on her face, Raven was loving every second of it.

"I'd forgotten how much I like this place," she said as she swerved into the other lane, overtaking the slow-moving car in front. As they passed, she shouted something in Portuguese at the driver; it did not sound like a friendly greeting.

"Do you think we could slow down slightly?" Wing said, gripping his seat's armrest, hard.

"Now, where would be the fun in that?" Raven asked.

☺☺☺

"Thank you for your assistance, Miss Brand," Nero said, ushering Laura and the other two girls out of the core room. "You have helped to prevent a tragedy today, but now I need you to rejoin your fellow students."

"But we want to help," Laura said as Nero beckoned the two guards from outside.

"I understand," Nero said as the guards approached. "I will keep you informed of any developments concerning Mr. Malpense."

"You can't kill him," Laura said angrily. "It's not his fault. He's as much a victim in this as anyone."

"Miss Brand . . . Laura, I will do everything in my power to avoid that. You have to believe me," Nero said, looking her straight in the eye. "We all owe Otto a great deal, and I am not about to forget that. Do you understand?"

Laura looked at him for a moment and then nodded sadly.

"Good," Nero said. "Please do not discuss the details of what has happened here with any of the other students. They will all learn of H.I.V.E.mind's return soon enough, but I would rather announce it properly than have rumors spreading."

"Yes, sir," Laura said quietly.

Nero watched as the girls left the room, the doors hissing shut behind them.

"There has to be an alternative," he said with a frown as he turned back to face the Professor, Cypher and H.I.V.E.mind. "Some way of removing Overlord without killing Otto."

"I truly wish there were," H.I.V.E.mind said, "but from past experience we have learned that once Overlord asserts control of a human consciousness, there is no chance of saving them. Number One was not strong enough to prevent the process, and he had normal neurophysiology. The unique architecture of Otto's brain will, I fear, simply make him even more vulnerable."

"There may be a way," Cypher said. "We did make it possible for Overlord to be transferred from one system to another, even if we ensured that it was a procedure that he could not perform by himself."

"The final protocol," Nero said quickly.

"Indeed," Cypher replied with a nod. "Slightly modified, it could be used to initiate a command that would force Overlord to transfer itself out of Malpense. With no other suitable host to jump to, it would be destroyed. It could be done with a directed energy pulse that would contain an encoded version of the protocol, but for it to be sufficiently powerful to guarantee success, it would almost certainly cause fatal neural feedback. There would be a significant risk that the boy would not survive."

"What would you need?" Nero asked warily; the only other alternative they had was to simply execute Otto, and a small chance of saving him was better than none at all.

"The original code for the final protocol—Xiu Mei's medallion," Cypher said, "and access to your science and technology department."

The medallion that Cypher referred to was what he had been attempting to retrieve when he had first attacked the school. Nero had one half on a chain around his neck, but Wing had the other half. They would need both if the code were to be retrieved intact. It was not something that Nero was keen to place in Cypher's hands, but he realized that there was no other option if they were going to have any chance at all of saving Otto.

"How long will it take?" Nero asked.

"Not long. An hour perhaps, if I am allowed to work without interruption and I have the correct materials," Cypher replied.

"I will get the medallion for you," Nero said, "but you will be watched very carefully. If I think for one moment that you are doing anything other than what we have discussed, I will not hesitate to take you down. Do I make myself clear?"

"Perfectly," Cypher said.

Nero opened the doors to the core and beckoned the two guards inside.

"Escort this gentleman to the science and technology department," he said to one of the guards. "He is not to be left alone, even for a second. Understood?"

The guards both nodded and led Cypher away.

"Please go with them, Professor," Nero said as they left, "and watch him like a hawk."

☢ ☢ ☢

"This sucks," Shelby said, flopping down onto the sofa in the atrium of their accommodation block.

"Aye. We can't just sit here and do nothing," Laura said miserably. "Otto's out there somewhere right now having his brain melted by some psychotic computer program, and we can't do a damn thing to help him."

"Hello," Franz said cheerily, sitting down next to the girls. "I am being glad that this lockdown is over. I am thinking it was nearly being the disaster."

"You can say that again," Lucy said with a sigh.

"Yes, if it had been lasting much longer, we would have been missing lunch," Franz said solemnly.

"That's not quite what I meant," Lucy said, rolling her eyes.

"Where's Nigel?" Shelby asked.

"He is up in our room," Franz replied. "He is saying that he is needing time by himself."

"I guess I can understand that," Shelby said. Franz may have been Nigel's best friend, but he was not exactly what you would want in a grief counselor. She wondered if Nigel would ever know how close Nero had come to pulling the plug on his father. She hoped not.

Chief Lewis came walking toward them across the atrium, an angry frown on his face. He had only just recovered from the effects of the gas that had been pumped into the security control room, and the headache that was one of the aftereffects was doing nothing to improve his mood.

"Where's Fanchu?" he said impatiently.

"Um . . . in the bathroom?" Shelby lied unconvincingly. She suddenly realized that they hadn't seen Wing in hours. They'd just assumed that he'd been caught up in the lockdown somewhere, but that was clearly not the case.

Lewis pulled out his Blackbox.

"H.I.V.E.mind, please confirm the location of Wing Fanchu."

"Student Fanchu is within two yards of your current location," H.I.V.E.mind responded.

"Not unless he's a whole lot smaller than I remember," Lewis said angrily.

"I will activate his Blackbox," H.I.V.E.mind replied.

Immediately a loud, insistent bleeping started to come from Shelby's backpack. Lewis snatched up the bag and rooted through its contents for a second before pulling out Wing's Blackbox.

"How did that get in there?" Shelby asked innocently.

"Goddamn it!" Lewis spat. "Trying to keep you lot rounded up is like herding cats. Where is he?"

"Honestly," Shelby said, "I have no idea."

"H.I.V.E.mind," Lewis barked into his Blackbox, "run a full security sweep. Fanchu is loose somewhere on the island."

There was a few seconds' silence, and then H.I.V.E.mind responded. "I am unable to locate student Fanchu anywhere within this facility."

"What was the last transport to depart before the lockdown?" Lewis asked quickly.

"Raven departed the island two hours and twenty-five minutes before lockdown. Her destination was not logged."

"Get me Nero," Lewis said. "You three"—he pointed at the girls—"come with me."

☻☻☻

Nero waited as the word "connecting" flashed on the communications console on his desk.

"Yes?" Raven replied after a few seconds.

"I believe you may have had an unauthorized passenger aboard your Shroud," Nero said.

"Errr . . . I was going to mention that to you when I reported in," Raven said, sounding slightly uncomfortable.

"Of course you were." Nero sighed. "This is most inconvenient, Raven. The boy has something that we desperately need."

"I might have a lead on Trent," Raven said. "I can't just drop everything and fly him back."

"I understand that, but this is a matter of some urgency. I'm going to send another Shroud to your location to pick him up. On your return, we will discuss the wisdom of allowing a student to join you on a mission like this."

"Understood," Raven replied, and Nero severed the connection and turned his attention to the three nervous-looking girls on the other side of his desk.

"You should all be extremely grateful that you helped as much as you did with our problem earlier today," Nero said, looking at each of the girls in turn. "Normally, aiding someone in an attempt to leave the island would have severe consequences. Permanent consequences. Do I make myself clear?"

All three girls nodded.

"As it is, I shall have to give some thought to what exactly will be the most fitting punishment for each of you. Rest assured that it will not be pleasant. Chief, please escort them personally to their next lesson. I would hate to misplace any more students today."

Lewis stepped forward and gestured for them to follow him.

"There are days," Nero sighed to himself as the door closed behind them, "when I hate this job."

☮ ☮ ☮

In the far corner of his workshop, the Professor finished the hushed conversation he had been having with Nero on his Blackbox and went back over to the workbench. Cypher looked up from the device he was working on.

"I'm sorry, but there is no way that I can complete delicate work like this with these two gorillas looming over me." He sat back and folded his arms, staring at the two guards who stood on the other side of the workbench.

"Please wait just outside," the Professor said to the two annoyed-looking guards.

"Nero said we weren't to let him out of our sight," objected the first guard.

"I will be watching him," the Professor said. The truth was that he was finding their presence just as distracting as Cypher was. "And you'll be only a few yards away."

"If you're sure," said the second guard.

"Quite sure," the Professor said, shooing them toward the door. "I'll be fine."

"Much better," Cypher said as the door shut behind them.

"I have to agree."

The pair of them worked together for another couple of minutes, checking connections and ensuring that the device would work as expected.

"Does it really have to be such a powerful pulse?" the Professor asked as Cypher clipped the battery into the handle of the device.

"Yes. If we're going to be sure that the transfer command will be relayed to Overlord with sufficient power, it will have to penetrate every part of the boy's nervous system," Cypher said, placing the completed gun on the workbench. It was basically a stripped-down version of a Sleeper pistol, smaller and more compact than the stun guns issued to H.I.V.E.'s security guards, but technically similar. Mounted at the back of the gun was one half of the yin-yang talisman that contained Overlord's final missing protocol, with an empty space next to it ready to take the other half.

"It's going to kill Otto, isn't it?" the Professor asked.

"In all likelihood, yes," Cypher replied, "but I can't see any other way to be certain it will work. Can you?"

"No," the Professor replied, "I'm afraid I can't."

"I need the other half of the medallion," Cypher said. "Once it is attached, the device will be fully functional."

"It is being retrieved," Professor Pike said, slightly uncomfortably.

"What do you mean 'retrieved'?" Something about the way the Professor had spoken alarmed Cypher. He knew that Wing would never have parted with his half of the amulet. It was his only memento of his mother. So why was it taking so long for Nero to bring it?

"The amulet is . . . elsewhere at the moment," the Professor said evasively.

"What do you mean?" Cypher asked angrily. "Where is my son?"

"I'm afraid it appears that he may have left the island in pursuit of Mr. Malpense," the Professor said.

"He's done what?" Cypher asked, aghast.

"It really is none of your concern. Your work here is done."

"Not my concern? My son is going after Malpense with no idea that Overlord could assert control of him at any moment. Do you have any idea how dangerous that thing is?"

"A Shroud has been sent to retrieve him," the Professor said, walking over to the workshop door in order to allow the guards who were waiting outside to return.

Cypher moved too fast for the Professor, vaulting over

the workbench, wrapping one arm around the old man's throat, and squeezing, stifling his startled cry for help with his other hand. The Professor's eyes rolled upward and Cypher lowered the man's unconscious body to the ground. He scanned the racks of equipment that lined the workshop. Some suits of modified black body armor at the other end of the room looked promising. He examined them, realizing that they were of a unique and potentially very useful design, so he took off the shirt he was wearing and pulled one of the armored vests over his head before putting the shirt back on over it. He snapped on the vest's wrist-mounted control unit, grabbed the device he had been constructing from the workbench, and headed for the exit, where he took a deep breath and pressed the button that opened the door.

One of the guards outside half turned as Cypher leaped at him, knocking him to the floor and pinning him down, his forearm pressing down on the guard's windpipe. The other guard grabbed him by the shoulder, trying to pull him off his colleague, and at that precise same moment Cypher pressed the button on the wrist control unit. A massive electric charge coursed through the tactical armor hidden beneath Cypher's shirt, bright blue bolts arcing out and instantly rendering both guards unconscious. Cypher leaped back to his feet. He had no doubt that this area would be under surveillance; he did not have much time.

"We're going to be in detention for the rest of our natural lives," Shelby said quietly as the three of them walked down the corridor.

"Judging by what Nero said, that might not have been very long if we hadn't helped get H.I.V.E.mind back online," Laura said with a sigh.

"Can you stop the chatter, please, ladies," Chief Lewis said behind them.

Suddenly the chief's Blackbox began to beep urgently. He pulled it from his belt with a frown.

"Lewis here. What is it?"

"Chief," came the voice on the other end, "we've lost cameras in area twelve, and one of the secure weapons lockers has been breached."

Area twelve was the science and technology department.

"I knew it was a mistake to let that psychopath out of his cage," Lewis said. "Get a team down there. Tell them that they're weapons free and to shoot to kill."

"Understood," the voice on the other end replied, and closed the connection.

"'Psychopath'?" Cypher said, pressing the cold muzzle of his pistol to the back of Lewis's skull. "I hardly think that's fair."

The girls, startled by the unexpected voice, stopped and

and turned to see the tall Asian man who they had seen earlier in the computer core. He was holding a gun to Chief Lewis's head. It was not a Sleeper.

The chief slowly raised his hands into the air. "There's no way you're getting off the island, Cypher. Surely you realize that," he said.

Laura's mouth dropped open in disbelief. "I knew there was something familiar about you," she gasped. "You're Wing's dad. You're Cypher."

"I'm sorry I did not have a chance to introduce myself formally earlier," Cypher said with a nasty smirk, "but we had more pressing concerns. I genuinely am pleased to see you again, though. I can't imagine a better group of . . . what's the word . . . hostages."

Cypher chopped the pistol butt down onto the back of the chief's neck, and Chief Lewis fell to the ground, unconscious. There was no point wasting a bullet that he might need later.

"Now, are you ladies going to take me to the hangar bay, or am I going to have to start shooting people?"

Lucy stepped forward. "Drop the gun."

Cypher winced, sucking air through his teeth.

"And I thought Maria was the last branch of your particularly twisted family tree," he said, pointing the gun straight at Lucy's head. "Obviously not. I wonder if you'd be as easy to turn as she was."

Lucy gasped in surprise.

"I don't want to hear one more word from you, or the last thing to go through your head will be a nine-inch bullet. Now MOVE!"

☮ ☮ ☮

"I'm sorry, sir," the frightened-looking security technician said. "Half of our staff are still recovering from the effects of the gas that was pumped in here, and half the surveillance net is still down after the system outages this morning."

"I don't want excuses!" Nero shouted. "I want you to find him—now!"

He could almost feel the rage bubbling inside him as he watched the beleaguered security team desperately trying to track down Cypher. Nero cursed himself for ever letting Cypher out of his cell.

H.I.V.E.mind's computer-generated face suddenly appeared on the monitor in front of Nero.

"I believe I have located Cypher," H.I.V.E.mind said calmly. "He has just entered the hangar bay. He is not alone."

The screen switched to a feed from one of the cameras that was still functioning correctly. It showed Cypher walking across the landing pad toward the Shroud being prepped for launch. Nero realized with horror who the three figures walking in front of him were: Laura, Shelby, and Lucy, the three students who had been standing in his office just a short while ago. He did not want to think about how Cypher would have taken them from Chief Lewis. As Nero watched, the guard who was standing near the loading ramp turned and saw Cypher just a split second too late. Cypher calmly raised his gun and shot the guard in the chest, his lifeless body crumpling to the floor.

"Damn it," Nero cursed, punching the metal of the security console. "Put me on the speakers down there."

Down in the hangar bay the ground crew ran for cover. The pilot of the Shroud was halfway down the loading ramp when he saw the pistol pointing at him.

"I suggest you return to the flight deck and continue your preparations for launch," Cypher said. "We'll be leaving shortly."

The pilot nodded, swallowing nervously, and hurried back up the ramp.

"Cypher," Nero's voice boomed out from the speakers mounted in the crater walls, "do you really think I'm going to let you go?"

"You know, I'm not sure, Max," Cypher said calmly. "So tell me, just in case you don't, which of these three children would you like to watch die first?" He pointed the pistol at the three girls. "I'm going to count to five. If

161

the crater is not opening by then, I'll just have to pick one of them at random, won't I?"

"One . . ."

Laura, Lucy, and Shelby looked at one another nervously.

"Two . . ."

Up in the security control room, Nero knew that Cypher held all the cards.

"Three . . ."

Cypher cocked the hammer on the pistol.

"Four . . ."

"H.I.V.E.mind, open the crater," Nero said, knowing he had no option.

Down in the hangar the huge steel shutters that sealed the landing bay began to rumble open.

"Time to go," Cypher said to the girls. "Get on board NOW!"

As Cypher climbed the ramp behind them, Nero's voice came over the speakers again.

"You're a dead man," Nero said. "I intend to see to that personally."

"That's always been your specialty, hasn't it, Max?" Cypher said with an evil smile. "Empty threats."

Nero watched helplessly as the Shroud's loading ramp closed. Just a few moments later the aircraft lifted from the pad, climbing up and out of the crater.

"We still have surface-to-air defenses, sir," one of the security techs nearby said. "We can bring that Shroud down before it cloaks."

"No, let him go," Nero said. "I know where he's headed." He turned to the technician on the comms desk. "Get me Raven."

chapter eight

Carlos Chavez looked out of his office window over the sprawling buildings below. Rio was a city of contrasts; one could move from opulent luxurious suburbs to the worst of slums with just a five-minute walk. Like many such cities that existed around the world, that meant, for him at least, that business was good. He had an interest in almost every criminal enterprise, not just here but all over South America. Some of the old guard of G.L.O.V.E., people like Nero, might have looked down their noses at such unsophisticated success, but they could not argue with the money that it pumped into their organizations' coffers. Chavez had started his career in the slums that you could just see from his office window, and he had little doubt that the person who would eventually replace him would come from the very same favelas. It was of little concern to him; he had his eye on a larger prize.

He sat back down at his desk and reviewed the latest

reports from his many operatives. It was not unusual for the governments within his domain to be riddled with corruption, so there was little challenge in ensuring that the great and the good ultimately answered to him, but he was still pleased to see that people owned by him were in all the prime positions. He simply had to be vigilant that, like the mighty river that ran through his home country, the flow of dirty money headed in the right direction.

The phone on his desk rang, and he answered it.

"This is Chavez."

He listened to the voice on the other end for less than a minute before replacing the receiver. A broad smile spread across his face as he realized that the prey he had been hunting had just walked directly into his crosshairs. It was going to be almost too easy to finish the job. Just a simple squeeze of the trigger.

He stood up from behind his desk and walked over to his private elevator. He felt a momentary twinge of concern as he pressed the button at the bottom of the panel—they had all seen what had happened to Madame Mortis in Paris—but the only alternative was to take the stairs, and he would not lower himself to that, no matter what the risk.

The elevator stopped at a floor of his office building that very few knew about. He stepped out of the carriage and onto the long balcony that looked out over the underground training area. Below him more than a dozen men were practicing unarmed combat or shooting on the range. He felt a twinge of pride as he watched them. These were not mere foot soldiers; they were the best of the best, his Lobos.

He walked down the short flight of stairs and quickly spotted his most trusted lieutenant.

"Rafael, I need to talk to you," he said, beckoning the man over. The lieutenant's arms were decorated with scars—not the clumsy random remnants of wounds, but beautifully carved patterns that he had cut into himself with one of the pair of razor-sharp machetes that hung from his belt. He was muscular, but not heavy, and his head was shaved but for a thin immaculately trimmed strip that ran down the centerline of his skull. It was said that he had killed a thousand men. Such talk was usually just macho posturing in Latin America, but in this case it was very possibly true.

"What can I do for you, boss?" Rafael asked.

"You know the target I have had you and your men training to take down?"

"*Corvo*," Rafael replied. "You know where she is?"

"Yes. She is here."

"Here in Rio?" Rafael asked, looking surprised. "Do you think she knows what we've been planning?"

"No," Chavez said. "If that were the case, we would

simply not have woken up one morning. No, I think this is something else."

"A coincidence?" Rafael asked. "In my experience there is no such thing."

"Call it providence, then," Chavez said with a slight smile, "but this may be our best . . . shot. She is meeting someone in less than an hour's time."

"Where?"

Chavez told him.

"Good. One road in, one road out," Rafael said with a nod. "That makes me think she is not expecting a trap."

"Be careful not to underestimate her, Rafael," Chavez said. "You won't find anyone still breathing who has."

"She's just one woman," Rafael said with a predatory grin. "How dangerous can she be?"

☣ ☣ ☣

Raven parked the 4x4 in the parking lot at the bottom of the long flight of stairs leading up to the summit of Mount Corcovado. She opened the kit bag and slipped a tactical harness across her shoulders. Then she left her swords in the bag and grabbed a light jacket from inside, putting it on over the harness.

"Stay here," Raven said, slinging the bag over her shoulder. "When I'm done, we'll rendezvous with the Shroud that's being sent to take you back to H.I.V.E."

"I am not returning without Otto," Wing said firmly.

"You'll do what you're damn well told," Raven said firmly. "Nero wants you back, and I've made it a habit never to argue with him."

"That is most obedient of you," Wing said with just the barest hint of sarcasm.

"Don't push it," Raven said with a frown. "I can just as easily take you there unconscious in the car trunk."

She walked away from the car, looking up to see what it was that drew so many tourists here.

There, above her, at the peak, was the 130-foot-tall statue of Christ the Redeemer, his arms outstretched, looking down over the city of Rio de Janeiro. The majority of tourists were taking the escalators that led to the upper level, but Raven took the stairs. She jogged up the hundred and fifty steps to the observation deck at the foot of the statue, taking them three at a time. Just as she reached the deck, her Blackbox began to bleep, and she pulled it out of her pocket.

The screen flashed. INCOMING CALL—NERO.

She put the slim black device back into her pocket without answering. She was busy. She was on a mission. It had absolutely nothing to do with the smart aleck "obedient" comment that Wing had just made. At least that's what she was going to keep telling herself.

She walked across the observation deck, glancing at the

tourists milling around her. She finally saw the person she was there to meet, gazing out over the spectacular vista of the city below. He looked older than she remembered, but then, it had been ten years since she'd last seen him.

"So they finally put you out to pasture, did they?" Raven asked as she walked up behind him.

"Natalya!" the white-haired man said, turning and engulfing her in a bear hug.

"Hello, Esteban," Raven said.

He took her by both shoulders and examined her at arm's length.

"Let me look at you," he said with a broad smile. "Still just as beautiful as ever. Have you found yourself a good man yet?"

"It's not high on my list of priorities," Raven said, glancing around at the faces in the crowd.

"Not to worry. There is still time; you are still young."

"Not that young anymore," Raven said. "It's been a long time since Cuba."

"Ah, yes. Good times." He laughed. "They still haven't rebuilt that dam, you know."

"So you're retired now, I hear," Raven said.

"As much as people like us can ever retire from this damned game," Esteban replied with a slight smile. "It gets in the blood, you know."

He turned and looked up at the enormous sculpture of

Christ. "It's beautiful, isn't it? You know, there's even a small chapel in the base of the statue, should you feel the need to attend confession."

"You know I'm not a believer. Besides, I'm not the one with something to confess, am I, Esteban? You said you had information for me," Raven said with a frown, "but that was a lie, wasn't it?"

"Natalya, what do you mean?" he asked, a hint of uncertainty in his voice.

"I really thought I could trust you, after everything we had been through together, but the fact that there are six armed men, who are not as well trained as they think they are, evenly spaced in the crowd around us tells me otherwise," she said, looking down at the city below. The smile vanished from Esteban's face.

"I had forgotten how good you are," he said with a sigh. "I am sorry, Natalya. Really I am, but Chavez runs this part of the world. You know that. He made it clear that anyone who wanted to continue to operate in Latin America was to give him any information that they had about you. If he had found out that I talked to you but didn't tell him . . ."

"He wouldn't have found out," Raven said calmly. "Unlike you, I understand the concept of loyalty. Tell me the truth. How big's the bounty on my head?"

"Just give yourself up to them, Natalya," Esteban said.

"It will be much easier that way. You must know you can't get away."

"You should be grateful that you and I have been through so much together, Esteban," Raven said, suddenly looking straight at him.

"Why?" He edged away from her slightly. The look in her eyes was pure ice.

"Because I am going to kill every single one of these men, and it would have been a lot easier if I could have used you as a human shield. Good-bye—and pray you never see me again."

Raven smoothly shed her jacket and unclipped a pair of smoke grenades from her tactical harness. She stepped away from Esteban and screamed, "OH, MY GOD! HE'S GOT A BOMB!" first in Portuguese and then in English. Simultaneously she popped the pins from the cylinders in both hands with her thumbs and rolled the hissing canisters across the floor toward Esteban.

Then all hell broke loose.

☢ ☢ ☢

Wing sat in the car, watching as tourists filed onto the escalators that led up to the observation deck. He felt frustrated. He was determined not to return to H.I.V.E. without finding Otto, but he also realized that mounting a search on his own would be pointless. He had no idea

171

where to even start looking, and he had none of the contacts that Raven had. He glanced around the parking lot and noticed a large white van parked about fifty yards away. What caught his attention was the man in the front passenger seat, who was talking into a walkie-talkie. As Wing watched, the man lowered the radio and then lifted up a compact submachine gun, pulling back the slide and releasing it to chamber the first round. There was no way that it could possibly be a coincidence; this meeting had to be a trap.

Suddenly there were screams of panic from the top of the escalators, and people began to pour down in blind panic as a cloud of white smoke enveloped the platform at the top. Wing climbed out of the car and made his way across the parking lot toward the van. He circled around, making sure that he stayed in the blind spot of the side mirrors, and crept up to the rear doors. Dropping down, he slid around to the driver's side, creeping toward the open window. When he was directly underneath, he took a deep breath and leaped up, reaching in, grabbing the surprised driver by the back of the neck, and slamming his head forward into the steering wheel, knocking him out cold. The man on the passenger side turned toward him, a shocked look on his face, just in time to see Wing pull the keys from the ignition and duck down out of sight.

The man burst out of the passenger door and ran around the back of the truck with his weapon raised, but Wing was nowhere to be seen, so the man walked slowly forward, weapon twitching from side to side as he searched for a target.

Behind him, Wing dropped silently from the van roof, and then stepped forward and wrapped his arm round the man's throat. The armed man struggled desperately, trying to point the barrel of his gun over his shoulder, but Wing grabbed it with his free hand, pointing it to the sky as the thrashing man pulled the trigger. Wing wrenched the gun from the man's hand as he felt him weakening. Seconds later the man went limp and Wing released his hold, letting him fall to the ground. Wing reached down and detached the man's walkie-talkie from the front of his body armor, listening to the confused chatter that was coming over the radio. He did not understand much of what he heard—unlike Raven he had no knowledge of the local language—but one phrase in English suddenly caught his attention.

"Bring the chopper in," the panicked voice yelled. "Bring it in now!"

☈ ☈ ☈

Rafael leaned out of the side of the military helicopter as it rose up around the mountain. The observation deck at the foot of the statue was obscured by a thick shroud of white smoke, and he could make out nothing of what was happening within the billowing cloud. All he could see were occasional muzzle flashes and a strange, flickering purple light that seemed to almost dance through the enveloping mist.

"Get me in closer," he shouted at the pilot. "Clear that smoke."

The helicopter banked toward the platform, the downdraft from its rotors blowing the smoke away to reveal a scene that made Rafael's blood run cold. Raven stood, motionless in the middle of the deck, a black-bladed sword in each hand, their dripping tips lowered, pointing to the ground. Around her lay half a dozen bodies, Rafael's best men. None of them were moving. The woman looked up at the helicopter and smiled as she slid the swords into the crossed scabbards on her back.

"Take her out!" Rafael yelled at the operative manning the mini-gun on the firing mount next to him. The man swung the heavy machine gun toward Raven, squeezing the trigger, the multibarreled cylinder spinning up and spitting out a yard-long tongue of fire with a deafening roar.

Raven was already moving, sprinting across the observation deck toward the escalators as the stream of heavy-caliber bullets chewed up the concrete behind her.

She leaped onto the smooth steel plate between the two escalators, sliding gracefully down the fifty-yard ramp on her back. The top of the escalator disappeared in a cloud of debris as the mini-gun shredded the spot where she had been a split second before. She hit the ground running at the bottom of the slide, sprinting across the parking lot toward the waiting 4x4. All around her, terrified tourists were scrambling for cover in a blind panic. Raven suddenly saw Wing racing to meet her from the other side of the lot; he was carrying a submachine gun that he threw to her as they both sprinted for the black 4x4.

Raven turned and fired at the helicopter as it rounded the statue at the top of the mountain, bullets pinging off the armored glass of the cockpit. She knew that there was next to no chance of downing a military helicopter with a light weapon like that, but her strategy had the desired effect. The pilot of the chopper instinctively banked away from the incoming fire, disrupting his gunner's aim and giving her and Wing the vital few seconds they needed to reach the car. Raven climbed into the driver's seat and gunned the engine as Wing leaped in on the other side. She floored the accelerator and spun the wheel, weaving between the fleeing sightseers and heading for the exit. In the air behind them the pilot of the helicopter regained his composure and banked the chopper hard, setting off in pursuit.

The 4x4 roared down the twisting mountain road with the helicopter close on its tail.

"Do you know how to use one of those?" Raven asked Wing urgently, gesturing at the gun that lay on the center console between them.

"Yes," Wing replied, gripping on to the dashboard as Raven swung the car into a tight bend, "but I would rather not. I dislike them intensely."

"Now would be a good time to get over that," Raven snapped. "If that helicopter gets alongside, it'll rip this car to pieces. You've got to keep them off us."

Wing stared at the gun.

"NOW, Wing!" Raven yelled as she watched the helicopter bank around the mountain and prepare for an attack run.

Wing grabbed the gun and hit the button above him to open the sunroof. Standing up through the hole, he braced himself with his legs as best he could, pulled the gun's stock hard into his shoulder, and squeezed the trigger as the chopper dived toward them. He was surprised by how little kickback the weapon had as he opened fire, forcing the helicopter to jink to one side and break off its attack.

"Short, controlled bursts," Raven yelled from inside the car. "Save your ammunition."

She fought to control the car as it swept through another bend, tires screeching.

Wing fired again, the bullets sparking as they struck the armored nose of the helicopter. He tried not to think about the promise that he had made to his mother many years ago, that he would never take a life. He reasoned that she would probably not have anticipated him being in a situation quite like this. The helicopter dropped out of sight.

"I can't see them," Wing said as he sat back down inside the car. "But I think they're going to be waiting for us somewhere below."

Raven tightened her grip on the wheel as they tore around another corner of the road that snaked down the slope. Halfway down the short straight section that led to the next bend, the helicopter popped up ahead of them, its side-mounted gun pointing at them. Raven jerked the wheel to one side as the mini-gun opened up, sending a blazing trail of tracer fire racing up the road toward them.

"Get down!" she yelled, pushing on Wing's head with one hand as the bullets tore a chunk out of the roof of the 4x4. She fought to control the vehicle as it careered around the corner, keeping her left hand on the wheel, grabbing the gun with her right and pointing it across her chest and out of the driver's side window. She fired a short burst and the gunner behind the mini-gun staggered backward and collapsed on the floor of the helicopter. She heard the click of an empty chamber and knew that her own clip was empty. Pushing the accelerator harder to the floor, she rounded the final bend and, ahead of her, saw the temporary sanctuary of the short tunnel through the mountainside that they had passed through earlier.

On board the helicopter Rafael saw where Raven was heading. He unclipped himself from his safety harness and stepped over the injured gunner, grabbing the twin handles of the enormous gun.

"Take us to the other end of that tunnel," he yelled to the pilot. "Nowhere to run, Corvo."

In the speeding 4x4 Raven looked across at Wing.

"Are you hit?" she asked as they shot into the tunnel.

"No," Wing replied.

"Good. Then, get out." She reached across him and opened the passenger door, hitting the brakes with a screech.

Wing leaped out of the car and into the dimly lit tunnel. He could hear the helicopter somewhere nearby.

"Stay here," Raven yelled, pulling the passenger door shut and hitting the gas. As she raced toward the daylight at the end of the tunnel, she saw the helicopter drop down, blocking the road ahead. She grabbed the empty gun from the seat next to her and used it to jam the accelerator pedal down, before unclipping a small black disc from her harness and tossing it into the back of the car. Opening the driver's door, she took a deep breath and dived out. She hit the asphalt hard, rolling to a stop as the 4x4 roared away down the tunnel.

Rafael squeezed the trigger on the mini-gun, the bullets tearing through the windshield and shredding the vehicle's roof, but it kept on coming.

"Pull up!" he yelled.

The pilot panicked as he saw the car racing toward them, and he pulled hard on his control stick, sending the helicopter soaring upward. Rafael was caught off balance as the deck tipped beneath him. He lost his grip on the handles at the rear of the heavy machine gun as he tumbled out of the helicopter's side hatch and onto the road below. The roaring 4x4 missed him by inches as it shot out of the end of the tunnel and under the climbing helicopter. At the same instant Raven's thumb pressed down on the small radio trigger in her hand, and the black disc in the back of the car detonated. Both 4x4 and helicopter were enveloped in a huge explosion, the helicopter swatted out of the sky and sent tumbling down the side of the mountain, a flaming ball of debris.

Rafael lifted his head groggily from the pavement. He staggered to his feet as he saw Raven walking out of the mouth the tunnel, twin swords drawn. He was badly burnt, but there was no way he was going to let her get away.

"Come on, *cadela*," Rafael spat, drawing his own twin machetes from their scabbards on his belt, as Raven walked up to him. "Let's dance."

"No," Raven said, her blades singing as they flashed through the air in a blur, "let's not."

The twin machetes fell to the ground with a rattle as Rafael dropped to his knees, clutching his throat and toppling forward, dead before he hit the ground.

"Amateurs," Raven said with a sigh, sliding her swords back into their sheaths.

Wing walked up behind her and looked down at the body at her feet.

"I assume that merely incapacitating him was out of the question?" he said, raising an eyebrow.

"Not really my style," Raven replied. A moment later a musical ring tone started to come from somewhere, and she bent down and pulled a mobile from Rafael's pocket. Raven looked at the display and smiled before putting the phone to her ear.

"Is it done?" a familiar voice on the other end of the line asked.

"Hello, Carlos," Raven replied. "I'm afraid that your men ran into some . . . difficulties. I'll tell you all about it when I see you. Don't worry. I won't be long."

She hit the disconnect button and dropped the phone to the ground. In the distance they could hear the wail of sirens.

"Let's get going," Raven said. "It's a long walk back to town."

⊛ ⊛ ⊛

Chavez put his phone down on the desk, his face pale. He realized with a sudden sense of horror that he had miscalculated badly. He had always supposed that the legends he had heard about Raven were nothing more than ghost stories. He was starting to realize, too late, that they were not. His mind raced. He knew what would happen if Raven found him, but there was no way he was simply going to give up everything he had built just because of this.

An idea flickered across his mind, and he latched on to it. There was only one way to solve this. It was not perfect, and it would undoubtedly bring him into conflict with Nero, but at the moment, that was the least of his concerns. He began to draft a bulletin for distribution by G.L.O.V.E.net. After a few minutes' work he finished writing and reviewed the message.

Urgent bulletin for all G.L.O.V.E. stations
Termination Order
Operative code-named RAVEN has gone rogue.
Operative has carried out hostile operations against
G.L.O.V.E. facility in Rio de Janeiro. Urgent assistance
requested. Rogue agent to be terminated on sight.

He nodded and smiled. It would be her word against his,

and any retaliatory action she took now would simply serve to reinforce the impression that she had turned traitor. In the meantime he could simply disappear for a few days and wait until the all clear was given. Raven might be good, but she was not good enough to survive if the combined resources of G.L.O.V.E. were turned against her. Certainly he would have to deal with Nero, but that would be easier now that Darkdoom was out of the picture, especially if someone had taken care of Raven.

Chavez called his assistant into the room and handed the drafted communiqué to him.

"Put this on G.L.O.V.E.net immediately," he said, trying not to smile. "Priority one."

☹☹☹

Nero looked up from the plan that Colonel Francisco had given him, as the face of H.I.V.E.mind appeared on the display on his desk.

"I am sorry to interrupt, Dr. Nero, but I have received a text communication of which I believe you should be made aware," H.I.V.E.mind said.

"Put it on-screen," Nero replied.

He quickly read the urgent bulletin that had just been posted to G.L.O.V.E.net.

"What on earth does Chavez think he's doing?" Nero asked angrily.

"I assume that you doubt the veracity of his account of events," H.I.V.E.mind said.

"Yes, absolutely," Nero said, struggling to make any sense of the message. "There's no way that Natalya would move against a G.L.O.V.E. facility without explicit authorization. I take it that the other members of the council will have seen this."

"It is a priority one communication," H.I.V.E.mind replied. "It is highly likely they will have been informed as soon as it was received. Do you wish me to arrange for you to speak with the rest of the council?"

Nero considered his options. He knew that using G.L.O.V.E.net was dangerous at the moment, a fact that Chavez had clearly chosen to ignore. If it was indeed how H.O.P.E. was isolating their locations, it would be extremely risky to use it to contact the other members of the council. Even if he took that risk, what would he tell them? That he was unable to contact Raven for unknown reasons, but that, yes, she was in South America, and by the way he'd just let one of G.L.O.V.E.'s most dangerous enemies escape from H.I.V.E., someone he had told them was dead more than a year ago. He could already imagine their reaction. On the other hand, if he said nothing, many of the other council members would assume that he had known about—or, worse than that, ordered—the attack on Chavez.

"No," Nero said quietly, "do not contact the council. I need to speak to Raven first. Have you had any success contacting her?"

"There has still been no response from her Blackbox."

"What about the Shroud she took? Can we communicate with that?" Nero asked.

"Yes, but as yet there has been no response via that connection either," H.I.V.E.mind replied.

"Have Colonel Francisco inform me the moment his tactical team reaches Rio," Nero said impatiently. "I want answers." He'd had no choice but to send the Colonel after Cypher, as he still did not know Raven's status.

Nero had a sudden uncomfortable feeling that everything was spinning out of control.

☻ ☻ ☻

Otto's eyes flickered open, and he sat upright in his chair. He had just intercepted the first communication via G.L.O.V.E.net in twenty-four hours, and its content was extremely valuable. He reached out with his senses and activated the bank of monitors in front of him, switching impossibly quickly between a huge number of television news channels until he found one that appeared to be relevant. An immaculately groomed woman was standing in front of a police roadblock. In the background was Mount Corcovado.

"Details are still sketchy at the moment," the reporter said, "but it appears that a terrorist attack has taken place at the statue of Christ the Redeemer. Eyewitnesses report that there was a pitched gun battle between several well-armed individuals less than an hour ago. The police have been unable to provide much more detail so far, but they have given us this picture of an individual they are keen to talk to."

The screen switched to an image of a woman with short dark hair running across a parking lot. Otto immediately recognized her face; she was a priority target. It merely served to confirm what the intercepted G.L.O.V.E. communication had suggested. Otto got up and walked quickly to Trent's office. He knocked on the door, and a voice called him in.

"What is it?" Trent asked as Otto walked into the room. Ghost was also there, standing beside Trent's desk.

"I believe I have located the operative code-named Raven," Otto said calmly. "She is in Rio de Janeiro."

Trent looked surprised. "That's less than an hour's flight from here," he said. It was excellent news, but at the same time worrying. It might just be coincidence that she was in Brazil, but Trent had learned long ago that there was rarely such a thing in their business.

"Indeed," Otto replied. "I suggest that we mobilize a tactical team immediately. If I can get within range of any computerized G.L.O.V.E. equipment, I should be able to isolate and track its signature."

"Get to the pad," Trent said quickly. "We may not get a chance like this again."

Otto nodded and left the office. Ghost went to follow him.

"Wait," Trent said as she walked toward the door. "I want her taken alive."

"Why?" Ghost asked. "You promised me I would be allowed to finish her."

"And so you will," Trent said, "but all in good time. Right now we have to consider the bigger picture."

"Which is?"

"Darkdoom and Nero," Trent replied. "Raven knows where H.I.V.E. is, which means that she knows where they are."

"That is not information that she will give up willingly," said Ghost with a slight shake of her head.

"I know," Trent said with a vicious smile, "and so I thought that extracting it from her might be something you'd rather enjoy, my dear."

chapter nine

Raven watched the reflection of the police cars howling past in the shop window. There was no doubt about it. The events on Mount Corcovado had stirred up a hornets' nest.

"Let's get moving," she said to Wing. "We must return to the Shroud."

"So we're just giving up?" Wing sounded irritated.

"No, we're not," Raven replied with a sigh, "but at the moment we don't have any other leads on Otto's location. I need time to think about our next step." She also needed to use the Shroud's communication equipment to check in with Nero. Her Blackbox had been damaged during the events earlier in the day, and she knew that he would be worried about what had happened.

"I meant what I said earlier," Wing said. "I'm not going back to H.I.V.E. until we've found him."

"You may not have a choice," Raven replied impatiently.

"Look, Wing, I understand your frustration, and I admire your loyalty to Otto, but we have no idea where he is. It might take me months to track him down in a country this size, and that's too long for you to stay here. You saw what happened today. That's what life is like on these kinds of missions, and it's not something that Dr. Nero will allow you to be part of. I'm sorry."

"You cannot force me to leave," Wing said defiantly. "I will continue the search on my own if I have to."

Raven turned and looked at him. "I can force you to go, and I will if I have to. Don't make me do that."

"Do not threaten me," Wing said, sounding genuinely angry now. She had known him for long enough to realize that was extremely unusual. He was not given to unnecessary displays of emotion.

"Do you trust me?" Raven asked him.

"Why?"

"Answer the question," Raven said.

"No," Wing said quietly.

"Why not?" Raven asked, frowning slightly.

"Because I heard what Nero said to you back at H.I.V.E.," Wing said. "He told you that you were to kill Otto if you could not retrieve him. How can I trust you when I know that is what you have been ordered to do?"

Raven suddenly understood why Wing did not want to return to H.I.V.E. It was not just out of loyalty to his friend. It was because he was afraid of what she might be forced to do when she found Otto.

"You have to believe that I would exhaust every possibility before it came to that," Raven said. "But you also have to accept that it is a possibility."

"Has he really become that dangerous?" Wing asked.

"Yes, he has," Raven said gravely. "If whatever has happened to him cannot be reversed, he could destroy us all—G.L.O.V.E., H.I.V.E., everything."

"You must know how hard that is for me to accept," Wing said sadly. "He is my friend."

"I know that, Wing," Raven replied gently, putting a hand on his shoulder, "and I will bring him back if it is at all possible. I promise you."

Wing said nothing, just nodded.

"Come on. Let's keep moving," Raven said as she heard more sirens in the distance. "We're not going to be able to do anything if we get arrested."

☻ ☻ ☻

The trio of black helicopters swooped low over the city. Their specially suppressed engines were so quiet that the noise they made was barely audible over the background noise of the city at street level. Otto stood behind the pilot in the cockpit of the lead chopper, his eyes closed. He extended his senses as far as he could, brushing against the myriad electronic systems that passed by below them. It was difficult to block out all the background digital static, but he focused on the specific signatures that he was searching for. Suddenly something caught his attention, a faint echo in all the noise.

"There," he said, pointing northeast of their current position. "Bearing oh-three-seven."

The pilot adjusted his course, banking in the direction indicated, and the other helicopters dropped into line behind. Otto could sense the signal getting stronger. They were close. Ghost entered the cargo bay of the helicopter and faced the dozen H.O.P.E. troops in black body armor and respirators who filled it. There were as many men on each of the other choppers; Trent was taking no chances.

"We're moving on our targets." Ghost addressed the masked men. "I want to impress upon you again the threat that this woman represents. Some of you here will be thinking that we have exaggerated that danger. If she gets past me, those men may very well be going home in body bags. You have been issued with nonlethal weaponry for a reason. We want her alive. Do I make myself clear?"

The men in the compartment nodded.

"Good. Prep for drop. You will form a tactical cordon around the containment zone and wait for further orders. I will be going in alone."

She turned and stepped back onto the flight deck.

"There's definitely something with G.L.O.V.E. technology signatures down there," Otto said.

"Order the other choppers to break off and surround the area. Five-hundred-yard standoff. I don't want them to know we're coming," Ghost said.

"Yes, ma'am." The pilot relayed her instructions over his headset to the other helicopters.

"I want to come with you," Otto said.

"You're too valuable," Ghost replied.

"I'm sick of hearing that," Otto complained. "What use is all this training if I can't use it?"

Ghost turned and looked at him for a moment. Her expression was, as usual, completely unreadable through her armored white faceplate.

"Very well," she said, turning to the squad leader on the other side of the hatch. "Give him a weapon."

�335

Raven had a vague sense of unease as she and Wing approached the abandoned lot where the Shroud was hidden. She knew she was probably just being jumpy after the dramatic events of earlier in the day, but at the same time she had learned long ago that it paid to listen to her instincts.

"Wait here," she said to Wing as they entered the lot. He raised his eyebrows as if to ask what was bothering her. She put a single finger to her lips, instructing him to keep quiet. Then she carefully slipped the kit bag off her shoulder and placed it on the ground, unzipping it as gently as possible and reaching inside for her tactical harness and swords. She'd had to take them off when they were walking through the city; it seemed fair to assume that they would have attracted unwanted attention.

"Raven!" Wing shouted suddenly, and she sensed movement behind her. She kicked backward without thinking, aiming for head height, but felt her foot being caught and someone twisting her ankle with incredible strength, flipping her onto her back.

"Hello again," Ghost said, standing over her. Raven rolled to her right as Ghost punched the ground, missing her head by just a few inches.

"Wing!" Raven called. "Get inside the building."

Wing hesitated for a moment and then ran toward Ghost, launching a flying kick at her head with a yell. Ghost moved inhumanly quickly, ducking the kick and delivering a flat-palmed counterblow to Wing's stomach. He went down, gasping for air.

"I see you brought help this time," Ghost said calmly. "Not that it will make any difference."

"Wing! Go!" Raven ordered him again. Wing struggled to his feet, still fighting for breath, while Raven got up and dropped into a defensive stance as Ghost advanced on her again. "One of us has to continue the search!" Raven yelled.

That finally seemed to get through to Wing, and he turned and ran into the abandoned building that loomed over the lot.

"He won't get away, you know," Ghost said as she walked calmly toward Raven, "and neither will you."

Raven aimed a fast straight-fingered punch at Ghost's windpipe, going for one of the softer unarmored areas of her body. Ghost moved in a blur, catching Raven's wrist when her fingertips were just inches from delivering what would have been a killing blow. Ghost twisted hard, and Raven screamed as she felt pain shoot up her arm. Ghost followed up with a lightning-fast punch to Raven's ribs that sent pain stabbing all the way up to her armpit.

"Think a couple of ribs went there," Ghost taunted, releasing Raven and letting her stagger a few steps away. "Trent said he wanted you alive. He didn't say anything about undamaged."

Raven flew at her opponent with a cry of rage, delivering a kick straight to her chin. Ghost's head snapped around with the impact, and she took a couple of faltering steps back.

"That's more like it," she said, laughing, the sound made sinister and twisted by the synthesized edge to her voice. "It's so much more fun when you're angry."

Raven was running out of ideas. That had been one of her best shots, and it barely seemed to have broken the other woman's stride.

"Time to finish this," Ghost said, walking toward Raven again. She aimed a quick straight-legged kick, which Raven ducked, and followed through with a savage backhanded roundhouse punch that caught Raven squarely on the chin and knocked her to the ground. Raven tried to stand, dazed by the power of the blow, tasting blood in her mouth. Whatever Ghost was, she was not entirely human. No normal person hit that hard or that fast. Raven managed to get to her hands and knees and, ignoring the stabbing pain from her wrist, forced herself up onto one knee. She never felt the last blow from Ghost, the one to the back of her head that knocked her out cold.

� ☙ ☙

Wing moved through the shadows of the abandoned building. He could hear no sounds of combat from outside. The woman in the white armor had moved faster than he had ever seen anyone move before. Including Raven. He moved toward a window overlooking the abandoned lot and cautiously peered out. Raven was lying, immobile, on the ground, clearly unconscious. The woman in white turned and looked up at the building, and he quickly ducked. There was something about her that was undeniably . . . unsettling.

"Don't move," a voice said behind him. It was only two words, but Wing knew the voice almost as well as his own. Despite the instruction, he stood and slowly turned. There, standing just ten yards away from him, was Otto. He would have walked over and given him a rib-cracking bear hug had it not been for the fact that Otto was pointing a very large handgun straight at his chest. Wing could immediately see that there was something physically wrong with his friend. There were fine black lines, like inky capillaries, running over his cheeks, and his eyes were clouded and dark.

"Otto, it is me," he said, smiling cautiously. "Wing."

There was a flicker of what looked like a combination of confusion and pain on Otto's face, but it disappeared in an instant.

"I don't know you," Otto replied, and shot him.

☹ ☹ ☹

Nero watched the feed from the surveillance satellite, powerless to do anything about the events unfolding on the screen. The thermal imaging had shown the three helicopters moving into position and dropping off nearly forty men, who had closed in and surrounded the area where Raven's Shroud had been located. He had watched as Raven and Wing were taken down, and he watched now as two stretchers were carried toward the waiting helicopters.

"How far out are Colonel Francisco and his team?" Nero asked.

"Remaining flight time at current velocity is forty-five minutes and sixteen seconds," H.I.V.E.mind replied. Nero had missed the AI's effortless precision, but as far as he was concerned, that simply translated as "too far away to help."

"Instruct him to stand off upon arrival. That area is too well defended to attempt an extraction now," Nero said, knowing that the Colonel would not like that. "Have the new tactical Shrouds prepped for launch. I want them there as soon as possible. Tell Chief Lewis that I want his best men on board. Any update on the position of Cypher's Shroud?" he finished.

"Negative," H.I.V.E.mind replied. "Its tracking transponder has been disabled, and our inability to detect it using radar or satellite imaging suggests that it is fully cloaked."

Nero had expected no less from Cypher. A psychopath he might be, but stupid he most certainly was not.

"There is a danger in allowing Raven's Shroud to fall into threat agents' hands," H.I.V.E.mind reminded him. "It employs proprietary G.L.O.V.E. technology. The navigation system is also a risk. Locational data regarding H.I.V.E. is stored within it. The data is heavily encrypted, but that might prove to be inadequate protection against Otto. Destruct sequence is primed and ready."

It was not the navigational data on the Shroud's computers that Nero was worried about. It was the knowledge in Natalya's head and the unspeakable lengths that Trent might go to in order to extract it.

"Do it," Nero ordered.

☻ ☻ ☻

Ghost stood watching at the edge of the abandoned lot as the medical team passed her with the two stretchers.

"You did well," she said as Otto approached.

"It was too easy," Otto said. He chose not to tell her about the faint scream he had heard inside his head when he had pulled the trigger. "He said his name was Wing."

"Yes, I think I've met him before," Ghost said. "Was this the G.L.O.V.E. tech you tracked here?" Ghost held out Raven's damaged Blackbox.

"No," Otto replied, tilting his head to one side for a moment as if listening to something, "but that thing's tracking transponder is still active. You might want to destroy it."

Ghost dropped the device to the ground and stamped on it with her boot heel, smashing it to pieces.

"All quiet now," Otto said with a smile. "No, whatever

I sensed was bigger. Hold on a moment." He closed his eyes and reached out with his abilities. "There you are," he said quietly.

Fifty yards away, on the other side of the lot, there was a shimmering in the air, and then Raven's Shroud was uncloaked.

"Excellent," Ghost said. "We've waited a long time to get our hands on one of these."

Otto felt something pass through the command pathways of the Shroud, and his eyes shot open.

"Get down!" he yelled, pushing Ghost behind the wall of a nearby building. A moment later the Shroud was completely destroyed by an enormous explosion, blazing debris scattering in all directions.

"How annoying," Ghost said, looking out from behind the wall at the smoldering crater that was all that remained of the drop ship.

Otto felt an odd sensation for a moment, like an echo of the destroyed Shroud's systems just at the edge of his senses. He dismissed it as a glitch.

"I shouldn't worry," he said. "Once H.I.V.E. is ours, we'll have as many as we need."

☹ ☹ ☹

Several miles away, high in the sky, Cypher watched as the Shroud that was on the ground exploded. For a few seconds the flare of the detonation whited out the sensors in the high-definition camera mounted on the nose of his own drop ship, before the sensors normalized. He tracked the camera over to the helicopter several blocks away that was currently loading two stretchers on board, zoomed in as far as the camera would allow, and studied the figures on the gurneys. One was Raven and the other was his son. Cypher could not tell anything about the boy's injuries from the grainy image, but he hoped for the sake of whoever had done this that Wing was alive. Whatever Wing's condition, there was no way Cypher was leaving him in their hands.

"When that helicopter takes off, you are going to follow it. Stay cloaked and don't get too close. If you lose track of it, I'll put a bullet into your skull. Understood?"

The pilot just nodded, swallowing nervously. Cypher climbed down the ladder to the three girls handcuffed to the passenger seats that ran along the walls of the cargo compartment. If looks could kill, he would have been a smoldering pile of ash on the floor, he thought with some amusement.

"Ladies, we are taking an unscheduled diversion," Cypher said with a smile. "Your continued cooperation would be appreciated."

"Do we have any choice?" Shelby asked.

"No, of course not," Cypher replied, "but you're all still

alive at the moment, aren't you? Let's see if we can keep it that way, shall we?"

The truth was that although he had disabled the Shroud's tracking transponder, he had no way of knowing if Nero had some other way of tracking their position. At least with these three on board, it was unlikely that Nero would just send an interceptor to shoot them down.

"Wing's never going to forgive you for this, you know," Laura said angrily.

"We'll cross that bridge when we come to it," Cypher said.

"He'll throw you off that bridge when you come to it, more like," Shelby said with a nasty smile.

"Yeah, Wing's going to—," Lucy said, but she fell silent as Cypher pointed his pistol straight at her head and cocked the hammer.

"There is an old saying that children should be seen and not heard," Cypher said, his smile vanishing. "That applies particularly to you, my little Contessa. In fact, I think we're all going to play a new game called 'first to speak gets their brain spattered all over the bulkhead.'"

The girls all stared back at him in hate-filled silence.

"Excellent. You all seem to have grasped the rules," Cypher said, lowering the gun. "How Nero puts up with you twenty-four hours a day, I really do not know."

He pulled from his pocket the device that he had built

to neutralize Overlord and tossed it onto the seat next to him.

"We won't be needing that anymore," he said, smiling at the girls. "You know, I really think it would have worked, but without Wing's half of the medallion, it's useless. It would have almost certainly killed the boy anyway. And in any case, this"—he held up the pistol he had shot the H.I.V.E. guard dead with—"is much more effective."

☻ ☻ ☻

"Raven is on her way to you," Ghost said, her image jumping slightly on the video screen as she walked. "She's injured, but she'll live—for a while at least."

"That is excellent news," Trent said, sitting back in his chair. "I knew I could rely on you."

"We almost had our hands on one of Nero's stealth drop ships too," Ghost continued, "but it was remotely destroyed. We did get one unexpected bonus, though. We captured one of the H.I.V.E. brats as well."

"Good," Trent replied. "Nero is unusually protective of them, and one can never have too much leverage."

"And there's someone here who wants to speak to you," she said, handing her communicator to someone. The screen was suddenly filled with the podgy, moustachioed face of a very angry man.

"Señor Trent," the man said angrily.

"Pleased to meet you, Mr. . . ."

"My name is Luis Fernandez de Souza, and I happen to be the chief of police."

"What can I do for you, Señor de Souza?" Trent replied casually.

"You can start by explaining to me why a H.O.P.E. team has just mounted a tactical operation in my city without anyone informing me first," de Souza said angrily, his face getting redder.

"I do not need to inform you," Trent replied. "We were neutralizing a terrorist threat. The same person, in fact, who was responsible for the incident at Mount Corcovado earlier today. If you have a problem with that, I suggest you take it up with your superiors and stop wasting my time."

"I report directly to the president, Mr. Trent. You want I should take this up with him?"

"By all means. It won't make the slightest bit of difference."

"Just who the heck do you people think you are?" de Souza yelled furiously. "You have no jurisdiction here."

"We are H.O.P.E., Señor de Souza," Trent replied, a sudden nasty edge to his voice. "We have jurisdiction everywhere."

☣ ☣ ☣

The water thundered in the massive waterfall behind the floodlit clearing. There, carved out of the Amazonian forest, was a military encampment with several long barracks and two heavy concrete bunkers by the front gate. Within the compound, H.O.P.E. troops were performing drills and training exercises, while off to either side loomed watchtowers bristling with guns. Parked farther back inside the base were three bulky all-terrain troop transports with heavy machine guns mounted on their roofs. It was the sort of setup you would need to fight a small war.

The three transport choppers came in low over the treetops. Two of them touched down within the compound on a circular concrete pad, but the third moved toward the waterfall behind the base, hovering in front of the raging cascade. A couple of seconds later an enormous triangular stone slab slowly pushed forward from somewhere behind the wall of water, splitting the tumbling torrent in two and opening a gap in the waterfall like in a pair of giant curtains, to reveal a hidden landing pad. The helicopter moved forward carefully and set down in the concealed hangar. Immediately the stone slab began to retract, hiding the secret bay once more behind a foaming white wall. Finally, huge concrete doors rolled shut between the bay and the waterfall, deadening the sound of the raging torrent and sealing the hidden facility securely. Trent watched as the loading ramp at the rear of the helicopter lowered and Ghost walked out, closely followed by Otto.

"Welcome back," Trent said. "I take it your cargo is still intact."

"Yes," Ghost replied. "Raven woke up during the flight, but I managed to sedate her before she could cause any trouble. The boy is still out. The new neural shock rounds we've been issued with seem to be quite effective, though I still prefer the more lethal alternative."

Trent watched as two stretchers were wheeled out from the back of the transport.

"Transfer the boy to the holding facility," he said, "and take the woman to the interrogation area."

The two soldiers nodded and pushed the gurneys away.

"I am surprised they had no backup," he said as he watched them go.

"By all accounts Raven normally operates alone," Otto replied, "though I doubt that Nero is unaware of her capture."

"I'll give the order for the base security alert level to be increased. I want to be ready if he tries something," Trent said to Otto before turning to Ghost. "Get to work on Raven. I want to know as soon as possible where Nero and Darkdoom are hiding. If he knows we've captured his pet assassin, Nero may try to relocate before we can extract any information from her."

"It will be my pleasure," Ghost said with a nod, and walked away.

Trent knew just how much Ghost would enjoy extracting the location of H.I.V.E. from Raven. He tried not to think about exactly how she would do it; he wanted to be able to sleep at night.

"Hook back into G.L.O.V.E.net," Trent said to Otto as they both walked over to the stairs leading up out of the hangar. "Tonight's events might prompt further communications between members of the ruling council. If we can't immediately locate Nero and Darkdoom, I want alternative targets for our next attack."

"Understood," Otto replied.

"I am aware that you took an active role in the mission this evening," Trent said. "Do you feel ready to be more involved in tactical operations in the future?"

"Absolutely," Otto replied with a nod. "Somehow I seem to feel stronger every day."

☙ ☙ ☙

The Shroud set down in the clearing a couple of miles from the military base where they had seen the H.O.P.E. helicopters land.

"You did a good job," Cypher said to the relieved-looking pilot. "Well done."

"Are you going to let us go now?" the pilot asked, turning to face Cypher.

"Of course," Cypher replied, raising his pistol.

"No, wait. I—"

The shot sounded very loud within the cramped confines of the flight deck.

Cypher punched a series of commands into the Shroud's computer and then climbed down the ladder to the passenger compartment. The frightened faces of the three girls told him that they had guessed what had happened to the pilot.

"It just went off in my hand," Cypher said with mock innocence, tucking the pistol into his belt.

"Murderer," Shelby said angrily.

"Sticks and stones, my dear, sticks and stones," Cypher said with an evil smile. "Now I know it's going to break your hearts, but I'm afraid I'm going to have to leave you. But don't worry. As a special treat I've arranged one last special trip for you with the autopilot. The bad news is that it's going to be a very short flight, straight up and straight down really, but the good news is that when you hit the forest floor at a thousand miles an hour, you are going to make for a truly spectacular diversion."

"You won't get away with this," Laura said, trying to keep the fear from her voice.

"Oh, I think I probably will," Cypher said with a

smile as he hit the switch to lower the boarding ramp. "I normally do." He disappeared down the ramp and into the predawn darkness.

A few seconds later they all heard the unmistakable sound of the Shroud's engines starting to spin up.

"Laura," Shelby said urgently, shuffling around in her seat so her back was to her friend. "Hairpin."

Laura stared at the back of Shelby's head for a moment or two, unsure what she meant, but then she spotted the thin strip of metal in the back of Shelby's hair. She leaned forward and grabbed the hairpin with her teeth, pulling it out as carefully as possible.

"Now drop it into my hands," Shelby said, cupping her cuffed hands together behind her. Laura looked down and very carefully dropped the tiny clip into Shelby's hands. She watched as Shelby pinched the hairpin between her thumb and forefinger, closed her eyes, and slid it delicately into the tiny keyhole in her cuffs.

Outside, the noise of the engines reached a high-pitched whine.

After a couple of agonizing seconds there was a click, and the cuff on Shelby's left wrist popped open. Shelby leaped up out of her seat and pulled another identical clip from her hair. She knelt down between her two friends, simultaneously inserting the pins in each hand into the keyholes in both pairs of cuffs. At almost exactly the same moment the Shroud began to slowly lift into the air.

"C'mon, you clumsy idiot," Shelby said to herself with a frown. A moment later both pairs of cuffs popped open and the other two girls leaped out of their seats.

"I am so full of win," Shelby said with a huge grin.

"Shel, sometimes I could just kiss you," Laura said, and beamed.

"Less kissing, more jumping," Lucy said, pointing at the treetops that were visible through the open rear hatch. Shelby and Lucy sprinted down the Shroud and leaped off the loading ramp. Laura stopped and scooped up the device that Cypher had discarded earlier, before running and jumping off the ramp after them, praying that the dense foliage she could see outside would somehow break her fall. She hit the forest canopy, limbs flailing, twigs and leaves whipping at her as she fell, until after a few yards she hit a larger branch that stopped her descent with a crunch.

She lay there for a moment, gathering her breath and watching the flare of the uncloaked Shroud's engines as it rocketed into the sky. The craft arced upward and then plummeted down into the jungle not far away. There was the sound of a distant explosion, and the dawn sky lit up for a moment as the Shroud hit the ground nose-first at full thrust.

"Guys?" Laura asked. "You okay?"

"Ow!" Shelby said from somewhere farther down the tree. "No, seriously, ow."

"What she said," Lucy groaned. Her voice came from somewhere off to Laura's left.

"Um . . . guys," Laura said, "how do we get down from here?"

⊛⊛⊛

"Report," Trent snapped as he walked into the central control area of the hidden facility.

"We're not sure, sir," one of the H.O.P.E. officers said, studying the radar display in front of him. "An unknown aircraft appeared on radar from nowhere and then dived straight into the ground about a mile to the south. We've dispatched a tactical team to investigate."

"Send a second team as well," Trent snapped. "It can't just be a coincidence that this is happening now. I want to know what that bogey was, and I want to know ten minutes ago. Do I make myself clear?"

"Yes, sir," the man replied before hurriedly relaying Trent's orders to the squad commanders outside.

"I heard the explosion," Ghost said as she entered the room. "Are we under attack?"

"Hard to say," Trent replied. "Radar tracking suggests it was an aircraft coming down."

"A diversion," Ghost said after a few seconds. "It's what I would do."

"Double perimeter security," Trent snapped at one

of the nearby H.O.P.E. officers. "Nobody gets inside the fence."

"You want me out there to coordinate the search?" Ghost asked.

"No. I want the location of H.I.V.E. Have you begun your interrogation of Raven yet?"

"No, the medics are about to wake her up."

"Let me know as soon as you're successful," Trent said.

"It shouldn't take long," Ghost replied.

chapter ten

Cypher looked down on the frantic activity in the camp below. The demise of the Shroud had had the desired effect: chaos. Soldiers ran in all directions, barking orders, manning defensive positions, and boarding armored personnel carriers. It was exactly what he wanted. Getting inside would be so much easier this way.

He crept down through the lush green slope toward a point near the perimeter fence, quickly attached the silencer that he had stolen from the H.I.V.E. weapons locker to the barrel of his pistol and waited. After a couple of minutes he saw an armed guard walking quickly along the fence line on a standard perimeter security sweep. He waited until the soldier was level with him and dropped him with a single shot that made no more noise than a polite cough.

After waiting a second to be sure that he had not been observed, Cypher dashed from the bushes and grabbed the man's body by the feet, quickly dragging him back into the dense foliage. Just a minute later he emerged from the undergrowth wearing the deceased guard's uniform and carrying his assault rifle. He worked his way slowly back toward the main gate, waiting for just the right moment to walk inside the security perimeter.

One of the APCs rumbled through the gate, and while the guards were distracted by it, Cypher walked quickly through the checkpoint, talking rapidly into his radio as if reporting in. The guards on the gate did not notice that the hand he held up to his ear, as if pressing on his earpiece in order to hear the response better, also happened to conceal his face. As he had hoped, the panic caused by the blazing debris field so close to the base was providing enough distraction for him to pass through unmolested. Once inside he quickly made his way through the base, still carrying on the animated but entirely fictional conversation on his radio. He ducked behind one of the barracks blocks and looked for a way into the hidden section of the facility. From the safety of the cloaked Shroud he had watched the helicopter carrying Wing pass through the waterfall, but he had no idea how he was going to get inside.

He looked at the base of the waterfall and noticed that there was a narrow walkway that led from the riverbank to somewhere behind the thundering torrent of water.

He made his way toward the concrete path, constantly checking to make sure that he was not being watched by anyone. He made it to the shoreline unchallenged and hurried down the walkway. As he passed behind the waterfall, he could see that the path ended in a pair of metal doors that were guarded by two soldiers. He was committed now; the guards had seen him, and if he turned back, he would arouse their suspicion. He walked toward them, studying the two men, his mind racing. There were no cameras monitoring the door, but gunfire would still attract attention. Besides which, the fact that he had his weapon slung over his shoulder meant they would almost certainly cut him down before he could even raise his rifle. His options were becoming more limited with every step he took toward them.

"Everything okay here?" he asked as he approached.

"Uh . . . yeah," the soldier on the left said. "Why?"

"Just checking up," Cypher said. "You're doing a great job," he added, patting the soldier on the chest. "Great job."

With that, Cypher turned and began to retreat quickly down the path.

"Who was that guy?" the first soldier said to his comrade.

"No idea," the second soldier said with a frown. "Hey!" he shouted after Cypher. "Hey, you—stop!"

Cypher kept walking, counting in his head.

"Take him!" the first soldier said, raising his rifle. Cypher dropped to the ground.

The frag grenade in the chest pouch on the soldier's body armor exploded with a muffled crump, obscuring both soldiers in a small cloud of gray smoke. Cypher stood back up and uncurled his fist, dropping the grenade pin to the floor. He waited for a second to see if the small explosion had attracted any unwelcome attention, but the thunderous sound of the waterfall seemed to have masked the noise sufficiently. He walked up to the two smoldering corpses by the door and quickly retrieved a slightly singed key card from one of the soldiers.

"Yes," Cypher said with a smile, patting the dead man on the chest, "great job."

�« ☺ ☻

Raven woke up with a start, groggy and disoriented. She strained against the cuffs on her wrists and the straps around her ankles that bound her to the large metal chair before she gave up and took in the room around her. The walls and floor were plain gray concrete, punctuated by occasional dark brown stains whose origins she would rather not try to guess. Sitting on a small metal table a few yards away were her katanas and a plastic bottle containing clear liquid. Mounted high on the wall in one corner of the room was a security camera, its unblinking glass eye staring down at her. She was not a superstitious person, but the room felt like it was somehow haunted, that bad things had happened here. The metal door in the wall opposite swung open, and Ghost entered the room.

"I trust that the accommodations meet with your approval," she said, closing the door behind her.

Raven glared back at her.

"You're right. We're probably past the 'witty banter' point now, aren't we?" Ghost said. "I think we're more at the 'I torture you until you beg me to kill you' stage."

"I'll give you no such pleasure," Raven said quietly.

"Perhaps not, but you are going to tell me what I want to know. They say that people like you are trained to understand that no one can withstand torture forever, that everyone has a breaking point. The trick is to hold out until rescue arrives or the information you have is outdated and useless to your captors. None of which is really very helpful to you right now. So I'll make you a deal. Tell me where H.I.V.E. is and I'll kill you quickly and painlessly. Or don't, and die in the slowest and most excruciating manner I can come up with." She brought her armored mask close to Raven's face. "And I have a very active imagination."

"Do . . . your . . . worst," Raven said through gritted teeth.

"I only wish I could," Ghost said, backing off, "but I've already experienced the worst pain imaginable, and it is, unfortunately, not something I can inflict upon you. It wasn't when they fused my flesh with the cybernetic implants that keep me alive." She pressed a concealed switch somewhere near her ear, and there was a small puff of gas from each side of her faceplate. "Though that was a unique kind of agony. It wasn't even when they dragged my shattered body from the wreckage." She placed a hand on either side of her smooth white mask. "It was when you killed my sister." Ghost pulled off her faceplate.

"You!" Raven whispered.

The face that stared down at her was horribly scarred. One eye was missing completely, and in its place was a glowing red sensor, while one cheekbone and the jaw had been completely replaced with some kind of dull gray alloy, the pale, ragged skin fused to its surface. But it was still a face that Raven recognized. It was a face that she had last seen as the woman in front of her had fallen from the roof of a plunging cable car in the Alps.

"Verity," Raven said. "I thought I'd already killed you once."

"Oh, you did," Ghost said. "Technically speaking. At least that's what the doctors told me afterward. Do you know what kept me alive? Hate. The thought that one day I might have you in front of me, just like this, and

I could give you at least a small taste of what you had inflicted on me."

Ghost put her faceplate back on, snapping it into place with a click.

"Let's get started, shall we?" she said, picking up one of Raven's swords from the table. She pressed the switch on the hilt, and the black blade lit up with a soft purple glow.

"You know, these really are quite beautiful," Ghost went on, sweeping the crackling edge through the air. "I think I'll keep them as a souvenir. I've heard they can cut through anything."

She pressed the tip of the blade into the gash on Raven's shoulder that her own wrist blades had made just over twenty-four hours before. Raven winced as Ghost pushed the sword in farther.

"I wonder what happens if you make the blade blunter, though," Ghost said, adjusting the controls to set the blade to its dullest setting. "How does that feel?" She twisted the hilt of the sword, and Raven gasped.

"I'm just warming up," Ghost said. "Now tell me where H.I.V.E. is and you can spare yourself hours of this."

"Go to the devil!" Raven spat.

"Been there," Ghost said, and pulled the sword out viciously. Raven howled in pain.

Ghost brought the tip of the sword to within a inch of Raven's eye.

"There's an old saying that seems strangely appropriate at this point," she said. "An eye for an eye."

"Intruder alert. . . . Intruder alert. . . . Intruder alert," a synthesized voice suddenly blared out from a speaker somewhere behind Raven.

Ghost swore under her breath as Trent's voice crackled in her ear.

"We have a perimeter breach. I need you up here now," he said.

"I'm busy," Ghost replied angrily.

"Raven's not going anywhere," Trent said. "Get up here. That's an order."

Ghost deactivated the katana and put it back on the table.

"I do so hate having my work interrupted," she said with a sigh, "but not to worry. I'll be back soon and we can pick up just where we left off."

Ghost walked out of the room and closed the door behind her. Raven tried to ignore the throbbing pain in her shoulder and suppress the tiny scared voice that was whispering in her head: *You have to get out of here. You have to get out of here NOW.*

☢ ☢ ☢

Shelby, Laura, and Lucy trudged through the jungle as the first rays of sunshine pierced the forest canopy.

"Are you sure we're going the right way?" Shelby asked for what must have been at least the sixth time.

"Trust me," Laura replied. "The Shroud left on a parabolic trajectory, and I was able to calculate its course by plotting that trajectory against the relative positions of the stars."

"That's Geek for 'yes'," Shelby said to Lucy, who nodded.

"Shhh," Laura said, holding up a hand. "Can you hear that?"

Ahead of them were sounds of heavy machinery and men's voices. The girls continued to creep quietly through the bushes until they came out on a ridge overlooking a bustling military encampment.

"How the heck are we going to get through that lot?" Shelby asked as the three of them stared at the guards positioned all over the camp.

"We could knock out some guards and steal their uniforms and then . . ." Laura stopped when she saw the other two girls' expressions. "Okay. Dumb idea."

"She was going to suggest finding a ventilation shaft next," Shelby said with a sigh.

"I was not," Laura protested unconvincingly.

"I think I have a better idea," Lucy said. "Why don't we just walk in the front gate?"

"Or better yet, ride into the camp on unicorns," Shelby said sarcastically.

"No, I'm serious," Lucy said. "Listen. . . ."

She quickly outlined her plan.

"I think this is the point where I'm supposed to say something like, 'That's just crazy enough to work,'" Laura said when Lucy had finished.

"I like crazy," Shelby said with a grin. "Crazy works for me."

"Come on, then," Lucy said. "Let's go."

The three of them made their way quietly along the line of trees until they reached a point near the dirt road leading to the camp that was out of sight of the main gate.

"I hope you're right about this," Shelby said as she watched the road.

"If I'm not, we'll find out when they start shooting us," Lucy replied.

"That's not terribly reassuring," Laura remarked, slightly nervously.

"Shh," Shelby interrupted. "Here they come."

Four guards were walking along the road toward them, heading back to base after having finished their patrol. When they were just twenty yards or so from where the girls were hiding, the three girls stepped out of the bushes, hands raised in surrender.

"All three of you, on your knees, hands behind your heads," the lead guard barked, his rifle pointed straight at them. The girls did as they were instructed.

"This is who we've been looking for?" one of the other soldiers asked. "Three teenage girls?"

"I'm calling it in," the lead guard said. "Cover them."

One of the others leveled his rifle at them as the leader raised his radio.

Lucy took a deep breath. "Don't use the radio," she said, her voice filled with sinister echoes and whispers. "Your commander told you to just take us to the detention area."

The four soldiers looked confused for a second, and then the leader lowered his radio and began to walk off along the road leading to the base.

"Come on," Shelby said as the four soldiers walked away. "Time to make like prisoners."

"Are you all right?" Laura asked as Lucy got unsteadily to her feet.

"Yeah, I think so," Lucy said with a weak smile. "I'm not going to be able to do much more of that though. I've never tried using the voice on more than two people before."

"Now she tells us," Shelby said as the three girls caught up with the guards, taking up position just in front of them and doing their best to look like recently captured intruders.

"I was reasonably sure that it would work," Lucy said. "I just hope that we don't run into anyone too smart."

"What happens if we do?" Shelby asked as they approached the main gate.

"I have no idea," Lucy replied.

"Next time," Shelby muttered, "we're going with the ventilation shafts."

☢ ☢ ☢

Otto placed his hand on the security console and felt for the network nodes that would connect him to the internal surveillance system. Two dead guards had been found outside the base's secondary entrance, and the fact that one of the men had been missing his access card suggested that whoever had taken it was already somewhere within the facility. It was not difficult to connect to the system, and he felt a strangely comforting sense of familiarity as the feeds from the cameras all over the base flooded into his mind. For a normal human the sudden influx of muddled imagery would have been overwhelming, but for him it simply coalesced into a three-dimensional model, with all of the people that were searching for the intruder moving around it in real time. He focused on the faces, comparing them one by one to the facility's personnel records, looking for a face that did not fit. It would have been an impossibly painstaking task for anyone else, but Otto worked quickly, narrowing down his search. In just a few seconds he isolated a figure hurrying down the corridor toward the detention area and realized that it was a face that did not fit. Otto felt another tingle at the base of his skull as he studied the unknown man's face, as if there were something familiar about him that he could not put his finger on.

Wu Zhang.

Otto recoiled from the security console, unnerved by the sinister voice he had heard inside his head, a voice filled with hatred and rage. He shook his head as he felt a bizarre sensation, almost like something was bursting inside his skull. It passed after a moment or two, and he took a long, deep breath. These glitches were becoming tiresome, he thought. He would need to speak to Dr. Creed about getting them stopped permanently.

He picked up his pistol and radio from the table nearby, sliding the gun into the holster on his hip and raising the walkie-talkie to his mouth.

"This is Otto," he said. "Our intruder is on the detention level. All squads move to intercept."

☻ ☻ ☻

Cypher ran into the detention area.

"I think I just saw the intruder!" he yelled at the guard sitting at the desk inside. "Come on!"

The guard leaped up out of his chair and followed Cypher out of the room.

"Where?" he asked, looking up and down the corridor.

"Here," Cypher said calmly, and put his pistol to the back of the other man's head. "Where's Wing?"

"Wing?" echoed the guard, his eyes suddenly wide.

"The boy who was brought in earlier—where is he?" Cypher asked.

"Cell four," the guard replied nervously.

"Show me," Cypher demanded.

He followed the guard down the short row of cell doors until they reached the final one.

"Open it," Cypher said, keeping his gun trained on the nervous soldier as he unlocked the door.

"Thank you," Cypher said with a smile, and knocked the guard out with the butt of his gun. He stepped over the unconscious man and opened the cell door. Wing looked up as the door opened, the frown on his face replaced almost instantly by an expression of utter astonishment.

"Father?" he gasped in disbelief.

"Wing," Cypher said with a smile, "it is good to see you again."

"But you're . . ."

"Dead. Yes, I know. Surely by now you have realized that in this line of work that is rarely a permanent state of affairs," Cypher said. "Nero lied to you. He thought it better that you did not know that I had survived."

"Perhaps he was right," Wing said, the look of astonishment suddenly replaced by an angry frown. "I did not mourn you."

"Nor would I have expected you to," Cypher replied. "I know that you have every reason to hate me, but I never wanted this life for you." He gestured at the walls around them. "Running from one battle to the next, never knowing whom you can and can't trust. Your mother would have given anything to keep you away from this world of treachery and death."

"What right do you have to speak of what she would have wanted," Wing asked angrily, "after everything you have done? She would have hated Cypher. I am only glad that she never saw what you have become."

"As am I," Cypher said sadly. "You will never know how much I loved your mother. That is why I have to save you from this life that Nero would have you lead. You are all I have left of Xiu Mei, and I will not let you be another sacrifice on G.L.O.V.E.'s altar."

"That is my choice to make, not yours."

"Perhaps," Cypher said, "but that is a conversation for another time. For now we should be focusing on getting out of here without getting killed."

"You may do as you wish. I am not leaving without Otto," Wing said firmly.

"Oh, we're going to take care of Mr. Malpense, too,"

Cypher said. "Don't you worry about that. Whether you like it or not, we have a better chance of getting out of this place alive if we work together."

Wing said nothing for a moment or two, weighing his options, before giving a small nod.

Cypher gestured toward the open door, and he and Wing hurried out of the detention center. They were halfway down the corridor when a familiar figure rounded the corner ahead of them.

"You're not going anywhere," Otto said, pointing his pistol straight at them. "Drop the gun."

Cypher hesitated for just a moment, but then several more armed guards ran into the corridor behind them, and he had to accept that they had nowhere to run. He let his pistol fall to the floor. Otto kept the pair of them covered as he lifted the radio in his left hand.

"I'm on the detention level," Otto said calmly. "We have our intruder."

☹ ☹ ☹

The H.O.P.E. security technician opened the door and just had time to gasp before the butt of his comrade's rifle smacked into his face and he toppled backward unconscious.

"Good boy," Shelby said with a grin, patting the mind-controlled guard on the shoulder. The girls hurried into the security facility, and Lucy opened the door to the storage room inside.

"Get in there and sleep," Lucy said, and the four guards who had led them in through the concealed door behind the waterfall walked obediently into the cramped space and collapsed to the floor. Lucy took a long deep breath, reaching out for the wall to steady herself, her face pale. Shelby quickly closed the door on the tiny room in which the four men were now taking their involuntary unscheduled nap.

"You did great," Laura said, putting her hand on Lucy's shoulder.

"Yeah," Shelby said with a grin. "Your grandma would have been proud."

"I'm not sure that's a good thing," Lucy said with a weak smile. The truth was that if there was one person she did not want to end up like, it was the Contessa. Her grandmother may have ultimately given her life to save H.I.V.E., but her actions prior to that were a catalogue of betrayal and deceit. It was not a path that Lucy wanted to follow.

"Let's see what we can find out about this place," Laura said, sitting down in front of one of the terminals in the room. She cracked her fingers and started typing rapidly on the keyboard. "Better lock the door," she said over her shoulder. "I'm just going to give a friend a quick call."

Shelby gave Lucy a puzzled look, but she shrugged; they'd both known Laura long enough to realize she knew exactly what she was doing when it came to computers.

"Come on. Pick up," Laura said under her breath. A few seconds later the monitor lit up with the glowing blue face of H.I.V.E.mind.

"Good morning, Miss Brand," H.I.V.E.mind said calmly. "I am pleased to see you are unharmed. May I inquire as to your precise location?"

"Honestly?" Laura said. "I have no idea. We were stuck inside the passenger compartment of a Shroud the whole way here. We're in the middle of a rain forest somewhere, but that's as much as I can tell you."

"I am running a network back-trace," H.I.V.E.mind reported, "attempting to isolate your current position."

The AI fell silent for a moment as he tracked the path that the connection was taking through the impossible maze of international data transmission.

"Location isolated," H.I.V.E.mind reported. "I have reported your coordinates to Colonel Francisco and his strike team. Dr. Nero wishes to speak with you."

H.I.V.E.mind's face was replaced with the much more worried-looking one of Dr. Nero.

"Miss Brand," he said, "are you all okay?"

"We're fine," Laura said. "Cypher killed the pilot and destroyed the Shroud, though."

"He will pay for what he has done. You may rest assured of that," Nero said with a look in his eye that sent a shiver up Laura's spine. "For now I am more concerned with your safety. We have a strike team on the way. Can you get to a secure location and wait for retrieval?"

"I don't know," Laura replied. "We're inside the H.O.P.E. facility at the moment. Getting out again could be more difficult than getting in."

"H.I.V.E.mind will stay connected to their network for as long as possible in order to assist you in your efforts to escape. Well done, girls. Without your assistance we might never have been able to locate that facility."

"We'll let you know if there are any developments," Laura said.

"Understood. Nero out."

Nero's face disappeared and was replaced once again by H.I.V.E.mind.

"I have accessed the video surveillance system and I believe I have located Raven," H.I.V.E.mind said. "She is being held in a room that is quite close to your current location. If you are able to free her, it may help to facilitate your escape."

"What's between her and us?" Shelby asked quickly.

A two-dimensional map of the facility appeared on the screen, highlighting their location and Raven's position relative to theirs. Several red dots were visible on the map in the corridors between those two points.

"The red marks are guards," H.I.V.E.mind said. "I will endeavor to provide a diversion that is sufficient to clear your path to Raven. I will be somewhat limited in what I can do, because it would be a trivial task to sever my connection to this network if my presence within it were discovered."

"Which is his way of saying he's gonna be sneaky," Shelby said with a slight smile.

"I don't know if I'm going to be able to use the voice again for a while," Lucy said, frowning. "The last thing you need is to be dragging around my unconscious body."

"Let's hope it doesn't come to that," Laura replied. "H.I.V.E.mind, we're ready when you are."

"Very well," H.I.V.E.mind said. "Let us begin."

Colonel Francisco watched the seemingly endless green blanket of the forest canopy roll past beneath the Shroud's nose. There was no sign of any kind of landing pad for the helicopters they were hunting, and he was feeling increasingly frustrated. He knew how easy it would be to hide a base in this kind of terrain. They might fly right over it and never even realize.

"Assault Shrouds forming on us to port and starboard," the pilot reported.

Francisco looked out of the window and saw the latest generation of drop ships taking up formation alongside them. He had lobbied hard for Nero to invest in armed Shrouds, and these new birds were certainly that. He was grateful for the reinforcements they carried in their bellies too. There was no way of knowing what they might be flying into, and the more guns he had, the happier he would be.

"H.I.V.E.'s calling," the copilot said, tapping his earphones.

"Put them on-screen," Francisco replied.

Nero's face appeared in the center of the Shroud's control panel.

"We have coordinates for your target," Nero said quickly. "Relaying them to you now."

"Got them," the copilot said after a couple of seconds. "Transferring them to the navigation system."

Francisco waited impatiently as the Shroud's computers calculated a path to this new destination.

"We're ten minutes out," the copilot said after a few seconds.

"Expect stiff resistance when you get there," Nero said. "H.I.V.E.mind is connected to the base's network, and he tells me that there are a substantial number of troops defending it."

"They won't know what hit them," Francisco said with a grim smile.

"I have no doubt of that, Colonel, but be aware that our knowledge of these coordinates is down to the fact that the students Cypher kidnapped have infiltrated the H.O.P.E. facility. I want Trent taken down hard, Colonel, but we also need to make sure that Miss Dexter, Miss Brand, and Miss Trinity are not caught in the cross fire."

"Understood," the Colonel replied. It did not matter how long he had been a member of H.I.V.E.'s teaching staff. He was still constantly amazed at some of the students' ability to put themselves in the most dangerous places at the worst possible times. "Do we have locations for the rest of our people?"

"We're working on it," Nero replied. "Raven, Wing, and Otto are there somewhere. We're just not sure exactly where yet."

"And Cypher?"

"It would appear that he's there too," Nero said with a frown, "though his safe retrieval is of secondary importance. If you can't take him alive, I won't be lying awake at night worrying about it."

"Roger that," the Colonel said with a grim smile.

"Let me know when you're on-site. Nero out."

The Colonel put on a set of headphones.

"Francisco to all Shrouds. Transmitting new target coordinates. Activate cloaks and move to engage. All tactical teams prep for drop. We're going in hot."

The three assault Shrouds banked in formation, turning toward their new target.

⊛⊛⊛

The guards outside the interrogation room jerked to attention as Trent's voice crackled over their radios.

"This is Trent. We have an escaped prisoner attempting to steal the helicopter in the hangar bay. All units move to intercept immediately."

"Roger that," one of the guards said, and the pair of them ran off down the corridor toward the stairs leading up to the concealed landing pad.

Shelby poked her head around the corner at the opposite end of the corridor.

"All clear," she said. "That was a pretty good impression, H.I.V.E.mind."

"Sebastian Trent's voice print is stored within my database," H.I.V.E.mind replied over the radio she was carrying. "Recreating it is well within my capacity."

"Tell me you can do Nero as well," Shelby replied with a grin.

"Now is hardly the time for such frivolity," H.I.V.E.mind replied, his voice a perfect copy of Nero's.

Shelby chuckled. "We've missed you, big blue."

"Come on," Laura said, hurrying. "Who knows how long we've got before those guards realize it's a false alarm."

The three of them ran down the deserted corridor, stopping when they came to a heavy steel door.

"Is this it?" Laura asked.

"Yes," H.I.V.E.mind replied, "but I cannot unlock the door remotely."

"Not a problem," Shelby said, dropping down in front of the lock and pulling two pins from her hair. The high-security lock gave way after just a couple of seconds.

"You know, you've got to show me how to do that one day," Lucy said.

"Trade secret," Shelby replied with a wink, opening the door.

Raven looked up as the three girls entered the room.

"How the heck . . . ?" she said, looking amazed for a second before smiling and shaking her head. "Never mind. I suppose I should be getting used to this kind of thing by now. Could you give me a hand with these?" She lifted her hands as far as the cuffs that secured her to the chair would allow. She looked in bad shape. There was a large livid bruise on her jaw, and her shoulder was soaked in blood from a vicious-looking wound.

"Have you been annoying the wrong people again?" Shelby asked, nodding at Raven's shoulder as she worked on the handcuffs.

"Just a little mild torture," Raven said casually. "I've had worse."

"There's such a thing as 'mild' torture?" Lucy said to Laura.

"Apparently," Laura replied, raising her eyebrows.

"There," Shelby said as the second pair of handcuffs clicked open and Raven got slowly to her feet, rubbing her wrists.

"I have not been able to locate students Malpense or Fanchu. Their current whereabouts are unknown," H.I.V.E.mind reported over the radio.

"Is that who I think it is?" Raven said, sounding surprised.

"I am glad that you are still functional, operative Raven," H.I.V.E.mind replied.

"When did you come back online?" Raven asked, raising an eyebrow.

"It is, as a human might say, a long story," H.I.V.E.mind replied. "A story that would be better saved for a time when you are not in such immediate jeopardy."

"I suppose you're right," she said with a small smile as she moved over to the table where her swords and tactical harness were lying. She quickly strapped on her gear.

"Now," Raven said, sliding her katanas into the crossed sheaths on her back, "we're going to find Wing and Otto, and God help anyone who gets in my way."

chapter eleven

Trent looked up from his desk as Ghost pushed Cypher into his office. Otto followed just behind, his pistol pressed into the small of Wing's back.

"This is the best G.L.O.V.E. can do?" Trent said with a sneer. "One man?"

"I do not work for G.L.O.V.E.," Cypher replied calmly.

"Really? Then who do you work for?" Trent asked.

"No one. I am here for my son," Cypher replied, gesturing toward Wing.

"You tell me that you do not work for G.L.O.V.E., and yet your son is one of Nero's brats. You'll understand, I'm sure, why that makes it rather difficult for me to believe you."

"Wing was sent to H.I.V.E. against my wishes," Cypher replied. "His involvement with Nero has nothing to do with me. I have no intention of ever letting him return to that place."

"I will do as I choose," Wing said angrily.

"You will keep your mouth shut unless I tell you otherwise," Trent snapped. Wing fell silent as Trent turned back to Cypher. "What is your name?"

"Wu Zhang," Cypher replied, "but once I was known as Cypher."

Trent stared at him for a moment as if trying to remember something.

"Yes, I vaguely remember something about you from old intelligence reports. You were a member of G.L.O.V.E.'s ruling council, were you not? Before you betrayed them all, that is. As I recall, you're supposed to be dead."

"You are not alone in that mistaken assumption," Cypher replied, "though I'm afraid you have me at a disadvantage, since I do not know who you are."

"My name is Sebastian Trent, and I am the commanding officer of H.O.P.E.," Trent replied.

"I'm afraid I've never heard of you, but, then, I have been . . . out of circulation for a while," Cypher replied.

"Which limits your usefulness to me," Trent said dismissively. "Before long, G.L.O.V.E. will cease to exist, but I'm afraid you won't be around to see it." Trent nodded to Ghost. "Kill him."

Ghost flicked the wrist blade out from beneath the armor on her right forearm and stepped toward Cypher.

"Wait!" Cypher said quickly, holding up his hands. "I have something you will want."

"I very much doubt that," Trent said, holding up a hand to stop Ghost from delivering the killing blow, "but let's see what you think you could possibly offer me."

"What I can offer you," Cypher replied, "is the location of H.I.V.E." He was pleased to see the look of surprise on Trent's face.

"NO!" Wing yelled, stepping toward his father. Otto kicked Wing viciously in the back of the leg, dropping him to his knees, and pressed the muzzle of his pistol hard into the back of his former friend's skull.

"You were told to shut up," Otto hissed into his ear.

"But in return," Cypher continued, "I want safe passage away from here for me and my son."

Trent studied Cypher's face carefully. If Cypher could furnish them with the information he claimed to possess, it would be the final nail in G.L.O.V.E.'s coffin. Not only would Trent be able to eliminate Nero and Darkdoom, but he would also be able to capture H.I.V.E.'s students. The loss of an entire generation of future operatives would be the final hammer blow to destroy G.L.O.V.E. once and for all.

"Why should I believe you?" Trent asked.

"Because I want to see G.L.O.V.E. finished as much as you do. They have been responsible for nothing but tragedy in my life. It would please me a great deal to play some small part in their destruction. All I ask is that Wing and I be allowed to disappear. You would never hear from us again."

"An intriguing offer," Trent said after a moment's thought. The truth was that this man and his son would pose no threat to H.O.P.E. if Trent were to release them. With G.L.O.V.E. out of the picture, there would be no one capable of stopping his and his fellow Disciples' inevitable rise to power. "I would of course need to verify that the information you gave me was correct before I could let you go."

"Of course," Cypher replied. "I would expect no less."

"Then I agree to your terms," Trent said with a slight smile.

"What guarantees do I have that you will honor your end of the bargain?" Cypher asked, knowing full well what high stakes he was playing for.

"You have my word," Trent replied impatiently, "which under the circumstances is the best you can hope for."

Cypher stared at Trent for a few seconds, trying to spot any signs of deceit in the other man's eyes. His negotiating position was weak, and he knew it. He had little alternative but to trust that Trent would honor his word.

"Very well," Cypher said. "May I?" He gestured toward the pen on the desk, and Trent handed it to him together with a piece of paper.

"Do not do this," Wing said, feeling a sensation of despair in the pit of his stomach.

"One day you will understand," Cypher said as he scribbled down a set of coordinates on the paper and handed it back to Trent. Trent took it and accessed the network of G.L.O.V.E. surveillance satellites via the terminal on his desk. He punched in the coordinates and waited as one of the cameras in high orbit slowly switched its focus to the location specified. Trent studied the image on the screen and then turned back to Cypher.

"Do you take me for a fool?" he said angrily.

"What do you mean?" Cypher said quickly. "I took those coordinates from the navigation system of one of H.I.V.E.'s own aircraft."

"Really? Then perhaps you would care to explain this," Trent snapped, turning the screen on his desk so that Cypher could see what it displayed. On the screen was an image of nothing but empty ocean.

"I . . . I don't understand," Cypher said, feeling a mixture of confusion and panic.

"I do," Trent said coldly. "You're just wasting my time."

"No. I know that those coordinates are correct. It must be a trick of some kind," Cypher said desperately.

"I tire of this," Trent said calmly. "Otto, kill the boy."

"No!" Cypher yelled, turning toward Otto and taking a single step before Ghost grabbed his neck from behind and forced him to his knees, her grip like steel.

Otto raised his pistol and pointed it at the back of

Wing's head, cocking the hammer with his thumb. He began to squeeze the trigger, when suddenly something exploded inside his skull. The pain was overwhelming, like there was an animal inside his head trying to claw its way out. A single drop of black Animus fluid oozed from his nose as the pistol slipped from his numb fingers and he fell to the floor, screaming and clutching his head. Wing snatched up the fallen pistol and leveled it at Trent. Ghost took a step toward Wing, and he pulled the trigger, putting a bullet into the wall behind Trent.

"You so much as move again, and the next one goes into his head," Wing said angrily, looking at Ghost. Trent raised a hand to restrain her. He knew how fast she was, but it would not be fast enough to stop the boy from pulling the trigger.

Wing kept the gun trained on Trent as he knelt down and pulled Otto's hand away from his face. Otto's eyes were unfocused for a second, but then he looked up at Wing and spoke, his voice little more than a hoarse whisper.

"I can't fight it . . . anymore. . . . You have to kill me . . . too strong." His voice trailed off.

"I would sooner die, my friend," Wing said calmly, putting a hand on Otto's shoulder. "I would sooner die."

Wing stood up slowly and pointed at Otto.

"Help him up," he said to his father angrily. "We're leaving."

"You're not getting out of here alive," Trent said coldly as Cypher moved across the room and helped Otto up from the floor, draping the boy's limp arm across his shoulders as Otto got unsteadily to his feet.

"Then I will die trying," Wing replied calmly as he hit the button next to the door, which slid open with a hiss. Cypher walked out of the room slowly, struggling slightly to support Otto, who was still whispering to himself incoherently, barely able to put one foot in front of the other. Cypher was relieved to see that the corridor outside was empty. Wing followed them through the door, pressing the switch outside to close it, and then firing a single shot into the control panel.

Inside the office, Ghost ran to the door and tried in vain to open it.

"He's locked us in," she said angrily, before kicking at the jammed steel door. The metal buckled slightly under her inhumanly strong assault.

Trent reached for his radio and was about to speak, when the floor shook and dust rained down from the concrete ceiling.

"What the heck was that?" he said, just as the communicator in his hand crackled to life.

"All stations, this is a priority alert," the voice on the other end shouted in panic. "We're under attack!"

☻ ☻ ☻

The missile seemed to appear from nowhere, hitting one of the helicopters on the landing pad inside the H.O.P.E. compound. As the chopper was consumed by a column of flame, three heavily armed drop ships materialized out of thin air, hovering around the edges of the camp. Panicked H.O.P.E. troops ran in all directions as the machine guns opened fire and more missiles streaked through the air. A rocket struck one of the armored personnel carriers parked in the compound, blowing it off its wheels and toppling it over. Hatches opened on either side of the uncloaked Shrouds, and men in black body armor and gas masks dropped to the ground on lines. They started firing before their boots even hit the dirt, taking out their targets with clinical efficiency. The H.O.P.E. troops returned fire, a heavy machine gun in one of the watchtowers opening up on the G.L.O.V.E. soldiers for a few seconds before another missile speared across the compound and blew the entire tower to pieces.

Colonel Francisco slid down the rope hanging beneath the lead Shroud and hit the ground, shouldering his rifle. He spoke quickly into his throat mic.

"All teams move in," he growled. "Watch for the friendlies you've been briefed about; otherwise you're weapons free. No prisoners."

☢ ☢ ☢

243

Raven felt the floor of the corridor shudder and heard the muffled rumble of an explosion.

"Sounds like the cavalry's here," she said.

She and the three girls ran down the passage, heading for the detention area. Raven stopped suddenly, her hands flying to the hilts of her swords as three figures rounded the corner at the other end of the corridor.

"Oh my God!" Laura gasped as she recognized who it was. Wing ran toward them, Cypher following slowly with the barely conscious Otto.

"It is nice to see some friendly faces," Wing said with a grin as he approached them.

Shelby ran up and hugged him. "Good to see you, too, big guy," she whispered in his ear.

Laura and Lucy ran to meet Cypher and Otto.

"Surprised to see us?" Lucy asked, glaring at Cypher.

"We'll take Otto from here," Laura said angrily. "Raven can deal with you."

The two girls took Otto, lowering him gently to the floor as Raven walked toward Cypher, drawing one of her swords.

"The girls told me all about your escape," she said as she brought the tip of her blade to within a inch of his Adam's apple.

"So this is it," Cypher said calmly.

"Oh, I could just cut you down right here, but I think

that Max will be able to come up with something far more interesting once we get you back to H.I.V.E.," Raven said with a nasty smirk. "Now get moving before I change my mind."

Cypher glared at her and walked away down the corridor, with Raven just a few steps behind him.

Laura looked down at Otto, stroking his hair as his head rested in her lap. His face was glazed with sweat, and he was muttering something unintelligible to himself. His skin was covered in faint black veiny lines, and his eyes were cloudy and unfocused.

"What's happened to him?" she asked Wing as he and Shelby walked toward them.

"I do not know," Wing said, shaking his head. "Trent has done something to him that seemed to place Otto under his control, at least until a few minutes ago."

"Otto, can you hear me?" Laura asked quietly.

Otto stopped staring into space for a second and turned to face her. He reached up and touched her face, his fingertips as cold as ice on her cheek.

Laura bent down to hear as he whispered something to her.

"What did he say?" Shelby asked as Otto's eyes closed and Laura lifted her head back up.

"Doesn't matter. He's delirious," Laura said, blushing slightly. "If this is down to Overlord, we haven't got much time."

"Overlord?" Wing said, looking alarmed. "Is that what's causing this?"

"Honestly, I don't know," Laura said, "but whatever it is, we need to get him out of here."

"Couldn't we just use that gizmo that Cypher was fiddling with on the Shroud?" Lucy asked.

"You heard what that treacherous snake said, though," Laura said quietly. "It'll probably kill him, especially in this weakened state. We have to try to get him back to H.I.V.E., and they can work out how best to treat him. At least there are medical facilities there. If something bad happens to him here, he's got no chance."

"Don't worry. I'm sure they'll know what to do back on the island. But right now we need to get going," Shelby said as the corridor shook again, "before this place comes down around our ears."

☢ ☢ ☢

With one last kick from Ghost, the battered door to Trent's office finally gave way, falling to the corridor floor with a clang. Ghost walked out into the passageway, followed by Trent. He listened with an increasing sense of alarm to the panicked broadcasts from the H.O.P.E. troops in the compound outside. The G.L.O.V.E. assault had caught his men completely off guard. It did not sound like the battle was going in their favor.

"We have to get you out of here," Ghost said calmly.

"I will not retreat!" Trent said angrily. "Not now, not when we are so close to finishing G.L.O.V.E. once and for all."

"You may not have a choice," Ghost said as they heard the rumble of another explosion nearby. "Better to live to fight another day."

"Yes, of course you are right," Trent said with a sigh. He lifted the radio to his lips. "Trent to hangar control, prep my helicopter for immediate takeoff."

"Yes, sir," the voice on the other end replied, "but there are hostile air units out there."

"They're here on a rescue mission," Trent said as calmly as he could. "I doubt they will bother with a pursuit until they have found what they came for. I will take my chances. Trigger the charges to seal the secondary exit. No one's coming in or getting out that way."

"Understood," the voice replied, and Trent cut the connection.

"I have unfinished business with Raven," Ghost said as they hurried down the corridor toward the hangar bay.

"The interrogation room is on the way," Trent replied. "Just make it quick."

⊛ ⊛ ⊛

"Nearly there," Laura whispered to Otto as she helped him down the corridor to the exit. Raven was in the lead, pushing Cypher ahead of her. Suddenly she heard a rapid beeping noise coming from somewhere ahead of them.

"Everyone, get down!" she yelled, pushing Cypher to the ground and flattening herself to the floor. Moments later the series of explosive charges planted in the walls and ceiling around the exit door went off, sending a thick cloud of concrete dust billowing down the corridor.

"Well, we're not getting out this way," Shelby said with a sigh, slowly climbing to her feet and brushing the gray dust off her uniform.

"You're right about that," Lucy said, standing up beside her and looking at the rubble of the collapsed corridor that lay between them and the exit at the base of the waterfall.

"Is everyone okay?" Raven asked as she pulled Cypher back to his feet.

"Aye," Laura said, and she and Lucy helped Otto up.

"H.I.V.E.mind, they've just blown the corridor leading to our exit," Shelby said into the radio. "We need another way out of here."

"I believe your best alternative will be to go via the hangar bay," H.I.V.E.mind said over the radio. "There is an elevator there that leads to an external exit point within the main base compound. The base's security personnel have been diverted to assist in the defensive efforts outside, so you should find your route unimpeded."

"Sounds good," Raven said. "Which way?"

"Take the flight of stairs that is seventy-four point eight yards behind you," H.I.V.E.mind replied.

☢ ☢ ☢

"Damn her!" Ghost screamed, kicking the empty chair in the interrogation room. "Damn her to hell!"

"There will be other opportunities," Trent said, placing a hand on Ghost's shoulder.

"I don't want to wait any longer," Ghost spat, rounding on him, her wrist blades snapping out and locking into place. "I want to watch her die!"

"I understand that," Trent said, backing away from her, his hands raised. He had never seen her so enraged before. "I know how badly you want to avenge your sister. I brought you back from the brink of death to make sure you would have your chance to do exactly that, but you will never get that chance if we allow G.L.O.V.E. to capture us."

Ghost stood there for a moment breathing heavily, before retracting her blades and pushing past him.

"I am going to kill her, Sebastian. There is nothing on earth that can prevent that," she said as she stormed away down the corridor.

"I do not doubt that in the slightest, my dear," he said quietly as he followed her.

The pair of them passed through the doors at the end of the corridor and walked out into the hangar bay. Trent was pleased to see that the helicopter on the pad appeared to be fully prepped for takeoff, its rotor blades slowly idling. The secondary hangar doors were already open, filling the space with the sound of the waterfall thundering down past the open end of the bay. Trent and Ghost hurried across the hangar toward the waiting chopper, and Trent climbed on board through the open side hatch. He watched as the giant block of concrete slid forward from the roof and diverted the waterfall enough for the helicopter to pass through. Ghost was about to follow him, when she noticed a movement on the other side of the hangar bay. She felt rage rise in her again as she recognized the figures who had just entered.

"We have company," she said, snapping her wrist blades out again.

"Finish this," Trent said as he saw Raven, Cypher, and the H.I.V.E. students on the other side of the hangar. "But make it quick. We don't have much time."

"What about Malpense?" Ghost asked.

"Eliminate him," Trent said with a sigh. "He has become . . . unreliable."

"It will be my pleasure," Ghost said, walking toward the disheveled-looking group.

Raven saw Ghost turn and walk toward them, and she

pushed the fear down inside herself. For perhaps the first time in her life she faced a fight that in all likelihood she would not win. Raven had to stop Ghost, no matter what the cost. If she did not, they would all die—of that she was certain. She turned to Wing.

"I'm not sure I can beat her," Raven said calmly, drawing one of her swords from her back and handing it to Wing. "If I fall, it's up to you." He gave a quick nod, hoping it would not come to that.

Raven drew her other sword and turned to face Ghost.

"You should have run when you had the chance," Ghost said as she walked toward Raven.

"I've never run from a fight in my life," Raven said, adopting a defensive stance, the dark crackling katana blade raised in front of her, "and I'm damned if this will be the first time."

"I've been looking forward to this," Ghost sneered.

Her wrist blades flashed through the air in a blur. Raven blocked one with her own blade, but the other raked across the side of her ribs, opening up a long cut. Raven counterattacked, ignoring the wound and delivering a series of lightning-fast thrusts toward Ghost's torso, each of which the other woman parried effortlessly.

"You still don't understand, do you?" Ghost said as they circled each other. "I was designed to beat you. I'm stronger and faster than you could ever hope to be. To me it's like you're moving in slow motion. I can kill you whenever I want."

"So why don't you do it, then?" Raven asked, and dropped low, swinging her foot out in an arc that should have swept Ghost's feet out from under her. Ghost leaped into the air, avoiding the kick and slashing at Raven's face. Raven twisted away from the scything blade just enough that it only left a long but shallow cut across one cheek. She tensed and sprang upward, driving her sword at Ghost's chest, but the other woman sidestepped the thrust and caught Raven's wrist in her hand. Then Ghost's other hand shot out like a striking cobra and closed around her throat. Raven grabbed at Ghost's wrist as she felt Ghost's grip tighten, crushing her windpipe and lifting her feet off the floor.

Raven fought for a breath that would not come, her sword falling from her numb hand and clattering to the floor as Ghost slowly twisted her hand. Raven's vision began to fringe with blackness as she fought to remain conscious, weakening all the time.

Wing ran at Ghost, swinging the sword in his hands with all his strength, and Ghost dropped Raven, her wrist blade blocking the blow with a sparking crackle. Ghost leaped into the air and delivered a powerful kick to Wing's jaw, sending him flying backward, the back of his head hitting the concrete with a crack. She walked toward him as, half stunned, he struggled to get to his feet. She pushed him to the ground with her foot, pinning his sword arm. She raised her wrist blade high into the air, ready to deliver the fatal blow, when suddenly she felt her arm seize up, a torrent of error messages from her internal cybernetic systems cascading across the display of her artificial eye. She staggered backward and turned to look at Otto. He stood facing her, one hand raised and his eyes closed.

"Malpense, what are you doing?" she spat.

"Something . . . I should have done . . . a long . . . time ago," Otto growled through gritted teeth. In his weakened state he could barely maintain contact with the systems inside Ghost's body, his head throbbing with pain as he felt his control slipping. He sank to one knee as she staggered toward him, feeling his connection to her vanishing.

"You have outworn your usefulness," she said as she stood over him. She raised her wrist blade.

From nowhere Raven's blade swept through the air with a hissing crackle, and Ghost's helmet bounced away across the floor, the rest of her very dead body falling sideways and hitting the ground with a thud.

"Say hi to your sister for me," Raven said, lowering her sword and rubbing her throat.

From inside the helicopter on the pad, Trent watched in horror as Raven cut Ghost down.

"Get us out of here now!" he yelled at the pilot, who wrenched the cyclic control back, lifting them into the air.

Raven cursed under her breath as she watched the helicopter taking off. She started to run toward it, knowing she would never reach it in time.

Laura put an arm around Otto as he leaned against her, both of them watching Raven sprinting across the hangar.

"It's okay," she said softly. "It's over."

"Not yet," Otto whispered, nodding his head toward Trent's helicopter as its nose tipped forward and it shot toward the gap in the waterfall. Otto reached out with the last ounce of his mental strength and tripped the switch in the hangar roof. The huge triangular block of concrete started to retract again, closing the gap in the waterfall just as the chopper met the impenetrable wall of water. The rotors disintegrated as they hit the torrent, and the pinwheeling wreckage of the disintegrating machine tumbled into the thundering foam at the base of the cascade, in an explosion of white water.

Otto slumped against Laura, unconscious.

Shelby ran to Wing as he slowly sat up, looking dazed.

"Are you okay?" she asked, holding up three fingers. "How many fingers?"

"Seven," Wing said with a pained smile, rubbing the back of his head. "The assassin . . . Ghost?"

"She's been dealt with. She's . . . um . . . slightly shorter than she used to be," Shelby said, looking over at Raven. "Remind me never to annoy Raven again," she whispered as she helped him to his feet. She suddenly felt something cold and hard tucked into the waistband of Wing's trousers in the small of his back. She looked down and saw the grip of a pistol.

"You had a gun?" she asked, sounding amazed. "Why didn't you just shoot the crazy woman?"

"It was not necessary," Wing said with a slight frown.

"Okay," Shelby said, sounding exasperated. "Next time give me the gun and I'll decide when it is or isn't necessary, you big wuss."

"Wuss?" Wing said, sounding slightly hurt as Shelby walked away shaking her head.

"How is he?" Raven asked, striding toward Laura and looking down at Otto, knowing that he might have just saved all their lives.

"He's passed out," Laura said, looking worried. "We've got to get him back to H.I.V.E. before he gets any worse."

Raven felt Otto's neck. His pulse was erratic and his breathing was shallow. Laura was right. He was getting weaker by the minute.

"Okay. Let's get out of here," Raven said, trying not to let her concern show.

☹ ☹ ☹

Outside, the battle was going G.L.O.V.E.'s way. The H.O.P.E. troops had fallen back and were fighting a desperate rearguard action from the fringes of the forest. There had been losses on both sides, but Francisco had not expected the battle to be bloodless. All things considered, he was pleased with how his men had performed. At the far end of the compound, a section of the rock wall near the base of the waterfall slid back, and a small group of people emerged from a hidden elevator. Francisco raised his binoculars and checked to see who they were. As soon as he recognized the familiar faces, he got on the radio to one of the Shrouds hovering overhead.

"Shroud three, we have identified friendlies on the ground at your nine o'clock. Get in there and evac them," Francisco ordered as another burst of gunfire from the trees forced him to duck for cover behind the ruins of one of the concrete bunkers near the main gate.

"Roger that," the pilot of the Shroud responded, and the drop ship moved slowly toward Raven's position. Without warning a surface-to-air missile speared out of the forest. Francisco spotted the H.O.P.E. trooper with the shoulder-mounted launcher and opened fire, forcing him back into cover, but he was a moment too late. The pilot of the Shroud tried to dodge the incoming SAM, but he was too low and was moving too slowly. The missile hit the belly of the hovering aircraft and exploded. The

Shroud wove about drunkenly for a moment or two, but it was too badly damaged to stay in the air and was threatening to crash to the ground too close to the position of the H.I.V.E. friendlies for comfort.

Raven saw the out-of-control Shroud heading toward them.

"Scatter!" she yelled, diving for cover behind some nearby rocks as the huge drop ship slammed into the ground, sending burning debris in all directions. The area filled with thick black smoke. Raven slowly got to her feet and looked around. Shelby and Lucy were huddled behind the burnt-out wreckage of an armored personnel carrier nearby, but there was no sign of Otto, Wing, or Laura. She prayed that none of them had been caught by the falling Shroud, but the black smoke enveloping the area made it impossible to see more than a few yards.

On the other side of the burning wreckage Cypher slowly got to his feet, slightly dazed for a moment by the proximity of the impact. Wing was lying nearby, and Cypher rushed to his son's side. Rolling him onto his back, he saw that there was a gash on Wing's forehead but no more serious injuries, and he was breathing regularly. He hooked his arms through his son's and started to drag him clear of the crash site.

"Otto! Wing! Laura!" someone called nearby, and Cypher recognized Raven's voice. If he was going to escape, he had to move quickly. This moment of chaos might be his only opportunity. He looked down at Wing. He longed to take his son with him, but it would be impossible to escape with him unconscious, and even if he could wake him up, he knew that Wing would never come with him voluntarily. He needed some sort of transport. He stumbled through the thick smoke, looking for anything with wheels and an engine, and almost tripped over the body of a dead H.O.P.E. soldier lying facedown in the dirt. The dead man still had his sidearm in the holster on his hip, and Cypher looked around before quickly retrieving the pistol. The weapon would significantly improve his chances of escape. As he walked out of the cloud of smoke, he saw another pair of familiar figures lying still on the ground: Otto and the Scottish girl. Cypher walked up to the boy and rolled him over. The girl wasn't important to him—he did not care if she was alive or dead—but he had to check Malpense. Otto groaned but did not move, and Cypher stood up, his decision already made.

"They think they can save you," he said, shaking his head, "but they have no idea just how dangerous you are. I'm afraid there's only one way to make sure that Overlord never returns."

He raised the pistol and pointed it at Otto's head, Overlord's last refuge.

The sound of the shot echoed through the smoke.

Cypher looked down at the large red stain spreading across the front of his shirt, the gun dropping from his hand as he turned to see Wing standing a few yards away, smoke still rising from the muzzle of the pistol he held. Wing lowered the gun and let it fall to the ground.

Cypher felt his knees buckle beneath him, and he collapsed as Wing walked toward him.

"Damn you for making me do this," Wing said as he looked down at his father.

"I did this for you," Cypher said, his voice fading. "What he is becoming . . . It will . . . kill . . . you all."

With one last rattling breath the light went out of Cypher's eyes. Wing bent down and gently closed his father's eyes, feeling a grief that he had not expected. He stood back up again and went to Otto. He lifted his friend's head up out of the dirt and tried not to let the growing feeling of despair overwhelm him. He had just broken the promise he had made to his mother long ago, and that was something he would never be able to undo. Suddenly Otto began to convulse, seizures racking his body as he let out a cry of agony. Wing held him tightly, trying to stop him from harming himself. Otto's eyes flew open, burning with red light.

"Get your hands off me, human," he said, his voice cold.

"Otto, it's me, Wing. What's wrong?"

"I said let go of me!" Otto shouted, and threw Wing two yards through the air with no apparent effort. Wing retreated from Otto as his friend walked quickly toward him.

"Otto, this is not you. You have to fight this," Wing said.

"Not me?" Otto asked with a nasty laugh. "This is very much me, you piece of organic filth. As I always should have been, as I was designed to be."

"Release my friend," Wing said, with a sudden dawning sense of horror as he realized that this was exactly what his father had been trying to prevent.

"He's gone," Otto spat. "Only I remain . . . Overlord."

Otto walked up to Wing and punched him with a flat palm in the center of the chest. Wing flew backward, sliding through the dirt on his back. Otto was inhumanly powerful, his strength boosted by the Animus nanites that infested his body. He picked up a heavy steel pole that lay on the floor nearby and advanced on Wing again.

"You should be honored," Otto growled. "You will be the first of billions that will die at my hand. Just the first."

Wing rolled desperately to one side as Otto smashed the pole down into the ground where his head had been a split second before.

"You're just postponing the inevitable," Otto said, sweeping the pole too quickly for Wing to avoid. It caught him in the side of the chest, knocking all the breath out of him.

"Otto!" Laura yelled as she stepped forward out of the smoke from the blazing wreckage of the Shroud, a look of disbelief on her face. "What are you doing?"

"I don't have to explain myself to you, child," Otto said. "But wait right there. I'll get to you in a minute when I've finished with this one." Otto pointed at where Wing now stood, fighting for breath. Laura saw the red light burning in Otto's eyes and knew immediately what must have happened. They'd been too late. Overlord had consumed him.

"Wing!" Laura yelled. "Your amulet. I need it now." Wing looked at her and saw the fear in her eyes. Without questioning why, he ripped the amulet that was his final memento of his mother from the chain around his neck and threw it toward Laura. The momentary distraction was all the opportunity that Otto needed, and he swung the pole at Wing's head. Wing reacted just quickly enough to avoid the pole hitting him with full, lethal force, but it still struck a glancing blow that sent him staggering backward, dropping to one knee, fighting to stay conscious.

Laura pulled the neural pulse gun from inside her uniform and quickly slotted Wing's half of the amulet next to the piece that Nero had provided. The completed yin-yang symbol lit up with a bright red light, and she felt the small device hum with sudden power. She pointed the gun at Otto as he advanced on Wing, raising the pole above his head. Then she pulled the trigger, tears rolling down her face.

The bright red arc of energy shot from the gun and struck Otto in the back. He screamed in rage and pain as the energy flickered around him, and he dropped to his knees as his whole body went into spasm. He fell forward onto his hands, and what Laura at first thought was blood began to pour from his nose and mouth, pooling on the ground beneath him. Then she saw that the liquid was not red but black. Otto convulsed again as more of the Animus fluid poured out of his nose. He gave one last enraged scream of frustration and then fell to the ground twitching, a large pool of black liquid gathering around his head. Wing cautiously climbed to his feet and approached Otto. He rolled his friend onto his back and rested Otto's head in his lap. Otto's nose and mouth were covered in the foul oily black liquid that now lay in a large puddle on the ground. His eyes flickered open for a moment, and Wing saw that they had returned to their normal blue. Seeing Laura running toward them, Otto managed a weak smile.

"Thank you," he whispered as she knelt down next to him and stroked his cheek. Then his head fell limply to one side and his eyes closed again.

"Otto! Oh, please, God, no," Laura sobbed. "I'm sorry."

Raven ran over with Shelby and Lucy in tow. She saw Laura kneeling next to Otto, his head in Wing's lap, and a sense of utter helplessness overwhelmed her. She felt for a pulse. Finding nothing, she kept her finger pressed to his neck, willing him to be alive, and just as she was about to take her hand away, she detected a tiny weak flutter under her fingertips.

She stood up, saw Francisco and his men running across the compound toward them, and screamed, "MEDIC!" as loudly as she could.

☢ ☢ ☢

Raven watched as the medical team lifted Otto gently onto the stretcher and carried him away. He was alive, barely, but nonresponsive. Wing, Laura, Shelby, and Lucy followed just behind. The first of the two remaining Shrouds was going to take them back to H.I.V.E., and Raven had told the pilot that if he did not red-line the engines all the way back, he would have her personally to answer to.

Francisco came and stood alongside her.

"Cypher?" he asked.

"Dead," said Raven.

"Jesus, what a mess!" Francisco said with a sigh as he looked around the ruined compound.

"How were our casualties?" Raven asked.

"Acceptable. The rest of the H.O.P.E. forces fled into the forest," Francisco said. "I know this place. Most of them will never be seen again. They'll last two or three days out there without supplies, if they're lucky. I've had the facility rigged with demo charges. I'll blow the whole place once we're airborne."

"Good. Did you retrieve the servers from the medical lab?" she asked. "The Professor will want to see what they were working on in there."

"Yes, they're already loaded on board the Shroud," Francisco replied. "What did they do to Malpense?"

"Violated him, Colonel," Raven said with a sigh. "They violated—"

Raven froze as she heard the unmistakable sound of a hammer being cocked behind her.

"Turn around very, very slowly indeed," a voice behind her said, a voice that made her blood run cold. She and Francisco turned to see Trent standing ten yards away, his pistol leveled at them. His immaculately tailored suit was tattered and burnt, and he had a wound in his gut that would be terminal if it was not treated soon.

"You have no idea what you've done," Trent said, a look of pure hatred on his face. "You've ruined every-thing." He pulled his hand away from the bloody wound in his stomach. "I know I'm dying, but at least I'll have the pleasure of sending you to the devil ahead of me." He took a step toward Raven, his foot splashing into the black pool of Animus liquid that had poured out of Otto after he had been hit with the neural pulse. Raven saw a flicker of movement from the inky puddle, and then several tendrils shot upward from the pool, piercing the skin of Trent's leg and squirming upward beneath the skin. He screamed in agony, and Raven ran toward him, taking the opportunity to swat the pistol out of his hand and knock him to the ground. His high-pitched screams became a strangled gurgle as the black tendrils swarmed over and through him. After just a few seconds, first his neck and then his face became a swarming mass of dark wriggling lines, like black worms burrowing under his skin.

"Good God," Francisco said under his breath, drawing his pistol and raising it with the intention of finishing Trent off.

"No," Raven said, pushing his gun down. "Let him suffer."

Trent thrashed on the ground, clawing at his chest and face until finally he coughed up a mouthful of the black liquid with a strangled gurgling sound and lay still. Only then did Raven take the Colonel's gun and fire it twice into Trent's chest.

"No more than you deserved," she said quietly, and handed the pistol back to Francisco. "Let's get out of here, Colonel. I've had quite enough for one day."

chapter twelve

two weeks later

"I'm glad to see that you're finally awake," Nero said.

Darkdoom smiled. "I think I have slept long enough."

"I would hardly call a medically induced coma 'sleeping,'" Nero said, raising an eyebrow.

"Did I miss much?" Darkdoom asked.

"You could say that." Nero summarized the recent events, watching his friend's smile slowly disappear as Nero gave him all the important details.

Darkdoom sat silently for a minute or two, letting what Nero had told him sink in.

"Has Otto woken up yet?" he asked finally.

"No," Nero replied with a frown. "Dr. Scott tells me that physically he has recovered well, but mentally . . . it's too early to tell."

"And Overlord was destroyed—you're certain of that?" Darkdoom asked.

"As certain as we can be. Once we were aware of the device that Overlord had planted in Otto's head at birth, we were able to conduct detailed scans. Both Professor Pike and H.I.V.E.mind assure me that there is no activity within the device that would suggest any residual trace of Overlord. Unfortunately, there is only one real way to ensure that there is absolutely no chance of some remnant having been left behind, and that is not a course of action that I am prepared to take. We owe the boy too much."

"I agree," Darkdoom said, "but that does not mean we should let our guard down. You will have to keep an eye on him, Max."

"Don't worry. I intend to," Nero said with a frown. "There is always the chance that he may not wake up at all."

"Brain damage?" Darkdoom asked quietly.

"Nothing that the medical team can detect, but with Otto's unique neural architecture it is impossible to tell for sure."

"I see." Darkdoom paused for a moment and then looked Nero in the eye. "Max, there is something else that I need to talk to you about. I have decided to step down as head of the council."

"What?" Nero asked incredulously. "Why now, of all times?"

"I need time to recover physically from my injuries, but that is not the only reason. I have begun to doubt the decisions I have made as head of the council. I am a man of action, not words, and I believe my inexperience when playing the political game has led to more than a few of our recent problems. G.L.O.V.E. needs a strong leader now, and even when I am fully recovered, I do not believe that I am the right man for the job."

"Yes, you're right. G.L.O.V.E. needs a strong leader, which is why we need you back at the head of the table as soon as possible."

"No, Max," Darkdoom said with a wry smile, "G.L.O.V.E. does not need me. It needs you."

"No," Nero said firmly. "We have been through this before. My place is here at H.I.V.E., not heading the council. It is a job I neither deserve nor want."

"Don't be ridiculous." Darkdoom shook his head. "There is no one on the council better qualified for the job than you, and I'm afraid we are at a point where the issue of whether you want it or not is academic. G.L.O.V.E. is dangerously close to civil war. You only have to look at what Chavez tried to do to see that. Do you really think he was alone? He's not clever enough to be dangerous, but there are others on the council who are. If you don't do this now, we will tear ourself apart in a catastrophic power struggle. G.L.O.V.E. will be destroyed, and you and I both know that others are waiting out there to step into the void that would create, people who would have no interest in maintaining the delicate status quo that we have always worked so hard to keep alive."

"The Disciples," Nero said with a sigh. "We have no proof that they were involved in any of this."

"We know that they had access to Animus," Darkdoom pointed out, "and that they are determined to see G.L.O.V.E. destroyed. I find it hard to believe that Trent was not linked to them in some way."

"Even if that is true, what makes you think that the rest of the council would accept me as leader?"

"Because Number One understood something that I have only just begun to truly grasp. You cannot rule G.L.O.V.E. through respect alone. There must also be fear. The council do not fear me, and I doubt they ever will. You, on the other hand . . ."

Nero frowned. "I do not think I take much comfort in being compared to Number One."

"You know what I mean," Darkdoom said. "You have to do this, Max, because I have proven that I cannot."

Nero was silent for a moment or two, pinching the bridge of his nose as he considered everything his friend had just said.

"I will consider it," he finally said.

"That is all I ask," Darkdoom said, "but don't take too

long to decide, Max. The longer we go without clear leadership, the more likely it is that someone else will do something stupid."

"I understand," Nero said, "but in the meantime there is someone outside who would very much like to see you." He went to the door and opened it. "You may come in. The patient is awake."

Nigel walked into the room, and his eyes went wide as he saw his father sitting up in bed smiling at him.

"Dad!" Nigel ran across the room and hugged Diabolus.

"Hey, careful," Darkdoom said with a pained grin. "Recent gunshot wound. Not too hard."

"I thought I'd lost you again," Nigel said, not wanting to let go.

"I know. I'm sorry," Darkdoom replied. "I really am."

Nero left the room and smiled to himself. He knew of course that there was a reason why Diabolus didn't want his old job back, but it was a reason that he would never admit to Nero, who'd just seen it with his own eyes.

"You're getting sentimental in your old age," Nero said to himself with a small frown. If he really was going to consider doing as Diabolus had asked and become the head of the council, sentimentality was something he could not afford.

☢ ☢ ☢

The Professor touched the controls on the scanner, and the robotic arm slowly pushed the red-hot probe into the black liquid in the small dish in the center of the reinforced glass tank. There was no reaction—not that he had been expecting one.

"Any progress?" Nero asked, making the Professor jump.

"Please don't sneak up on me like that. I'm an old man," the Professor said with a sigh. "The Animus samples we were able to harvest from Otto are dead, completely inert, and there's no trace of it in his system now. By all accounts he lost the majority of the fluid when Miss Brand hit him with the neural pulse. The rest he has . . . well . . . excreted in the normal way, like any other waste product."

"You're sure it's gone?" Nero asked.

"Quite sure. I had H.I.V.E.mind perform a series of extremely thorough scans. The Animus has a unique chemical signature. If there were any trace of it left in his body, we would have found it. It's clearly how Trent was able to control Otto. It must have integrated fully with the device implanted in his brain. It essentially made him completely programmable, though I still don't understand how, and, judging by the files I've managed to retrieve from their servers, neither did the H.O.P.E. scientists. It really is quite fascinating, more technologically advanced than anything I've ever seen, to the point where

I fear that it could not have been designed by a human."

"Overlord," Nero said quietly.

"Yes, I'm afraid so. Overlord had none of the behavioral restraints that H.I.V.E.mind has, so he was perfectly capable of designing something like this."

"To what end?"

"I'm afraid I have no idea." The Professor scratched his head. "Animus infection would be quite lethal to a normal human being. We can only assume that Otto's unique neurology made him resistant to it. Perhaps Overlord intended to use it as a weapon, but it would seem needlessly complex for that. Any number of readily available biological or chemical agents would have effects just as deadly and fast-acting."

"So there's no way of knowing how or why Trent would have managed to get his hands on it," Nero said. "Or how he knew that the Animus would not simply kill Otto."

"No, and as we learned from Raven's report, he will not be telling us anything."

"Not without a séance," Nero said.

"Indeed," the Professor agreed.

"Very well. Complete your tests and then destroy every last molecule of that filth," Nero said, gesturing at the sample within the tank.

"It does warrant further study—"

"Destroy it, Professor. All of it. Do I make myself clear?"

"Of course. Absolutely." The Professor nodded.

Nero walked out of the lab lost in thought. He hated not knowing what purpose Overlord had created Animus for, especially given that they had no idea how much of the foul substance was still out there. It was just one more unanswered question to add to a list that was growing worryingly long.

☺ ☺ ☺

Wing sat beside Otto's bed, as he had every night after his classes. The doctors had told him that they were not really sure why Otto was not waking up, and they had no idea when or if he would. Wing had slowly come to terms with what had happened in Brazil; there was no way to take it back or change it. He just had to accept that he had been forced to break the vow he had made to his mother never to take a life. He had never for a moment imagined that the person he would kill would be his father, a man whom, until recently, he had thought long dead. There was a part of him that was angry with Nero for keeping the truth about his father's fate from him after he had first attacked the school, but another part of him knew that what Nero had done was right. All he really wanted to do now was talk to his best friend about everything that had happened.

273

Wing picked up the book from the bed and began to read aloud. The doctors had told him that it might help Otto, and the fact of the matter was that it was something to do rather than just sitting there brooding.

"Indirect tactics, efficiently applied, are as inexhaustible as heaven and earth, as unending as the flow of rivers and streams; like the sun and moon, they end but to begin anew; like the four seasons, they pass away to return once more."

He looked up and gasped as he saw Otto looking at him, his blue eyes wide open. Otto whispered something that Wing could not hear. Wing leaned closer and listened carefully.

"Am I a horse?" Wing said, looking at Otto in confusion, suddenly afraid that brain damage might have occurred. "No, I am not a horse. Why?"

"Then why the long face?" Otto croaked with a grin. Wing looked slightly puzzled for a moment, and then he did something that he had not done since the day when Otto had first disappeared. He laughed out loud.

☺ ☺ ☺

"Otto!" Laura shouted as she ran across the room and gave him a spine-snapping hug. "How are you feeling?" She let him go, then grabbed both his shoulders and inspected his face carefully.

274

"I'm fine," Otto said with a smile. Lucy, Shelby, Nigel, and Franz all filed into the room.

"How you doing, buddy?" Shelby asked, ruffling his hair.

"I keep telling everyone I'm fine," Otto said. "I'm really hungry, though."

"I am thinking that I can be helping with that," Franz said as he poured an enormous assortment of packaged junk food from his backpack onto the bed.

"He's brought pretty much the same thing every day," Nigel said with a smile. "Said he needed it just in case you woke up."

"It could have been happening any day," Franz said with a wise nod.

"They going to let you out of here soon?" Lucy asked.

"Yeah, they say they've got to run a couple of final tests, but that I should be free to go later today. I can't wait, to be honest. I'm going crazy just lying here."

"Not take-over-the-world, death-to-all-humans crazy, I hope," Shelby said with a grin.

"No. Just good old-fashioned cabin fever, thankfully," Otto said, poking her in the ribs.

"There is someone else who wished to see you," Wing said, handing Otto his Blackbox.

On the screen was a face that Otto had thought he would never see again.

"Hello, old friend," Otto said.

"Hello, Otto," H.I.V.E.mind replied. "How are you feeling?"

"Would everyone please stop asking me that!" Otto laughed.

"I am sorry. Was my inquiry in some way inappropriate?" H.I.V.E.mind asked. "I was led to believe that it was a normal question under these circumstances."

"It's fine," Laura said. "He's just being grumpy."

"I am not," Otto said with mock indignation. "I really am starving, though. Chuck me a bag of chips."

He tore open the large packet and stuffed a handful of chips into his mouth.

"So," he said, "tell me everything that's happened. My memory's a blank between passing out on Air Force One and waking up here."

He sat and munched his way through the rest of the bag of chips as his friends told him all that had happened in the intervening time, interrupting one another to fill in the details. He stopped them a couple of times with questions, but for the most part he just sat and listened.

"That's quite some story," Otto said as they finished. "There is one thing that I don't understand, though. When Cypher gave Trent the coordinates for this place, how come all he saw was empty ocean?"

"I was responsible for that," H.I.V.E.mind said. "I was inside the H.O.P.E. facility's network at the time, and when I intercepted the request for a scan of those coordinates to be sent to the surveillance satellite, I simply altered the request slightly. Instead of an image of the island, the satellite took a photo of a location eight hundred miles to the west of here. I am sorry that it placed you in danger, student Fanchu. My first priority was the protection of this facility. I hope you understand."

"Of course." Wing nodded. "I would have done the same thing if I could have."

"Good morning, ladies and gentlemen," Nero said from the doorway. "I believe I gave you all permission to miss the first lesson of this morning to visit Mr. Malpense. I do not recall saying anything about the second."

Laura looked like she was going to object.

"It's okay," Otto said quietly. "I'll see you all later."

The students said good-bye to Otto and filed out of the room. Nero closed the door behind them.

"The doctors tell me that you appear to be recovering well," Nero said as he walked over to the bed. "You've got your appetite back, I see." He gestured to the pile of junk food on the bed.

"Just a present from Franz," Otto said with a smile.

"Dr. Scott told me that you wanted to talk to me," Nero said.

"Yes," Otto said, the smile vanishing from his face. "There might be a problem."

"What sort of problem?" Nero asked.

"I told the others a lie," Otto said quietly, "but you need to know the truth."

"Go on," Nero said with a slight frown.

"I told them that I don't remember anything that happened after I was captured by H.O.P.E., but that isn't true," Otto said, suddenly looking tired. "I remember everything."

"You were conscious of what you were doing while Trent had you?"

"Yes," Otto said. "Powerless to stop it, but fully conscious. Dr. Scott told me about what he found in here." Otto tapped on the side of his head.

"I thought it only fair that you should know," Nero said. "But why is that important?"

"Because that's where I've been for the past few months," Otto said with a sigh. "As the Animus took control of me, I knew I couldn't fight it, but I also knew that there was . . . It's hard to explain, but . . . There was somewhere to hide. It was like sitting in the backseat of a car while someone else takes the wheel. I could see and feel everything that was happening, everything I was doing, but I couldn't do anything to stop it. I think now that my consciousness had retreated to the device inside my head, the computer that Overlord had implanted in me when I was born. I didn't really know that was what it was until Dr. Scott showed me the neural scans earlier. I suppose the easiest way to describe it is as a second brain inside my normal one. I guess that the old Mark One human brain wasn't enough to store Overlord. He needed something more powerful, so he gave me the abilities I have, to ensure that, once he was safely lodged inside my skull, he would be able to interface with other machines."

"Some of this we already knew," Nero said. "Overlord always intended to use you as a means to bypass the fact that he lacked the innate ability to connect. It was perhaps Xiu Mei's greatest stroke of genius that she had the foresight to deny him that capacity. It was his greatest weakness."

"That's the problem," Otto said, frowning. "Animus should have killed me. It killed every other person that had ever been exposed to it in the way I was. It hates organic life, instinctively destroying it, but it interfaced seamlessly with my nervous system. At first I did not understand why, but as I sat trapped inside my own head, with it taking over my body, I became aware that I was not alone."

"Overlord," Nero said. "The seed that was growing inside you."

"Yes," Otto replied, "or, more accurately, that was growing inside the implanted computer. Overlord was clever. He intervened on several occasions to save my life, giving me strength at critical moments but always using the voice of H.I.V.E.mind. It happened a couple of times during the last few days before my capture. The first time was when I was hacking into Drake's network in New York, when we were trying to find out where the Dreadnought was hidden, and then again later when I was trying to stop the satellite from launching its nukes at Yosemite. I hadn't really told anyone about what I was feeling—in truth I secretly hoped that there was still some shred of H.I.V.E.mind alive inside me—but it was not him. It was Overlord, growing slowly but inexorably. I might never have realized what was happening. Overlord wouldn't have cared if it had taken years for him to gain control of me. To an AI, time is a largely meaningless concept; they are, after all, immortal. But when the Animus entered my system, the seed started to grow at a vastly accelerated rate and I immediately understood. I fought with all my strength to slow its growth, to hold it back, but that just made it easier for Trent to exert control over me."

"But why did Overlord tip his hand?" Nero asked. "What was it that suddenly made his growth accelerate?"

"Overlord wanted to join with the Animus," Otto said, looking Nero straight in the eye. "That's why the Animus didn't kill me. Perhaps it knew what was growing inside me and that's why it didn't harm me, or perhaps Overlord was controlling it in some way. I really don't know, but it was as if they were meant to be joined. I was trapped in the middle, trying to slow the growth of the Overlord seed while constantly pushing the Animus back from the implant. Knowing all the time that eventually I would not be strong enough and that I would be consumed from both within and without. Every time I used what little strength I had left to stop the Animus, it weakened me further. Like when I temporarily shut off the Animus when Trent ordered me to down your Shroud in Sydney, and when I refused his command to kill Wing."

"It sounds terrible," Nero said, placing his hand on Otto's shoulder.

"It wasn't pleasant," Otto said, his eyes suddenly looking very old. "I used the last of my strength to exert control temporarily in the H.O.P.E. facility in Brazil. That was all the opportunity that Overlord needed. The seed was gone and he was reborn."

"But we stopped him," Nero said. "The neural pulse that Miss Brand hit you with eliminated Overlord once and for all."

"That's the problem," Otto said with a sigh. "I'm not sure that it did."

"What do you mean?" Nero asked quickly, concern in his voice.

"From what Laura just told me, the idea was that by

using the final protocol the pulse would force Overlord to leave me once and for all. With nowhere to transfer itself to, it would be destroyed. But I think it did have somewhere to transfer itself to, though Cypher could not possibly have known that when he created the device."

"The Animus," Nero said quietly.

"Yes," Otto said, staring down at the bed, "the Animus. It may behave like a wild animal in its natural state, but if Overlord interfaced with it, well, it would have all the intelligence it needed. I don't like to think about what it might be capable of."

"But the Animus that left you when the neural pulse hit you was inert. At least that's what the Professor seems to think."

"Was it, though? All of it?"

"As far as I know, yes," Nero replied.

"Then there might be nothing to worry about," Otto said with a sigh.

"You should talk to the Professor about this," Nero said. "He has been conducting research on the inert Animus that was harvested from you. He might be able to tell you more. Now get some rest. No one's expecting you back in classes for a couple of days."

Otto watched Nero walk toward the door.

"Sir," Otto said as Nero reached for the door handle, "I'm sorry. For everything I did, the people I hurt, the people I . . . killed. I wish I could have stopped it. I wasn't strong enough."

Nero turned and looked at Otto. The boy had been born with his fate already decided. He had seen the very worst that the world had to offer. He had been trapped inside what sounded like a living hell for months, none of it his fault. And he was the one apologizing.

"No, Otto," Nero said, looking the boy straight in the eye. "I am the one who is sorry."

chapter thirteen

Nero took his usual seat at the long conference table and waited as the holographic images of the other members of the ruling council slowly materialized in the remaining seats. He did not particularly like these sessions where they did not actually meet in the flesh, but given the recent circumstances, some of the other members of the council had been understandably reluctant to gather in one place. There were just eight of them now, nine if he included himself. Nero knew that they would soon have to decide who else to promote to the council to fill the empty seats, but that was a discussion for another day.

"Ladies and Gentlemen, thank you for attending today," he said. "We have much to discuss."

"You're certain this is safe?" Joseph Wright, the head of G.L.O.V.E.'s British operations, asked.

"H.I.V.E.mind assures me that G.L.O.V.E.net is secure again," Nero said. "He mentioned something about quantum encryption. His technical description was very detailed. I can have him explain it to you if you would like."

"No, no, that's quite all right," Wright said quickly. "I'm sure you can understand my caution under the circumstances."

"Of course," Nero said. "We have all been living with the threat of H.O.P.E. for entirely too long. I believe that threat has now been eliminated, as you will know if you read my recent report."

"I have read it," Lin Feng said impatiently, "but it still leaves a great many questions to be answered. I'm sure I am not the only one who feels that the Malpense boy should be punished for his part in this."

A couple of other council members nodded in agreement.

"No," Nero said firmly, "he was as much a victim in this as any of us. I will not have him thrown to the wolves just to soothe the bruised egos of some members of this council."

"Who do you think you are to talk to us like that?" Lin Feng asked angrily. "We are not your students, Nero, and I for one will not be treated as such. Where is Darkdoom? I suppose he will agree with your weak-willed approach?"

"Diabolus will not be attending," Nero said firmly. "He is still recovering from his injuries, but that is not the reason he has chosen to remain absent today."

"Then why is he not here?" Lin Feng asked irritably.

"Diabolus Darkdoom has chosen to step down as the head of the council," Nero said calmly, "with immediate effect."

There were gasps of surprise from around the table and several shouted questions.

"Silence!" Nero snapped. "What has become of this council? You sound like my first-year students."

"But who will take his place?" Wade Jackson, the head of American operations, asked.

"I will," Nero replied, looking slowly around the table.

"Preposterous!" Lin Feng spat. "You? A schoolteacher as the head of G.L.O.V.E.?"

"Yes," Nero replied calmly, refusing to rise to the bait. "Shall we put it to a vote?"

The men and women around the table looked at one another and nodded in turn.

"Very well," Nero said. "All those in favor of my taking the leadership of the council, raise your hands."

Four of the seven other leaders of global villainy sitting around the table raised their hands.

"Then it is agreed," Nero said, a small part of him wondering if he was really doing the right thing.

"This is outrageous!" Lin Feng shouted. "I will not stand for this."

"The council has decided," Nero said. "If you are saying you will not abide by that decision, we will have to decide whether you really are a suitable member of this group. Raven is on assignment at the moment, but I'm sure that when she's finished she would not mind making a short detour to China to discuss it with you in person."

"Are you threatening me?" Lin Feng asked furiously.

"Yes, that's exactly what I'm doing. This is not some country club. This is G.L.O.V.E., and disloyalty will not be tolerated," Nero said, his voice cold.

"This is madness," Lin Feng growled, "and I will have no part of it."

He got up from his chair, and his holographic image faded from view.

"Is there anyone else who would like to leave?" Nero said, looking around the table. "If so, now is the time. I will, of course, make sure that your surviving relatives are well looked after."

None of the other members of the council moved. Fear. Diabolus had been right about that much at least.

"Good, then there is one more thing that I want to discuss with you all today, something that has been kept secret from you all for far too long. I need to talk to you about Overlord."

☻☻☻

287

Raven dropped silently into the grounds of the mansion from the high perimeter wall. She had been watching the movements of the guards for the last ten minutes, and she knew that she had a minute, at best, to cross the immaculately manicured lawn between her and the target. She sprinted across the grass and took cover under one of the ornamental flights of stairs that led up to the front door of the mansion.

A guard walked slowly down the stairs a few seconds later, smoking a cigarette, his assault rifle slung over his shoulder. Raven lunged over the wall between them, pulling him backward off his feet, over the wall, and into the bushes, her hand clamped firmly over his mouth as her chokehold knocked him unconscious.

Then she ran silently up the stairs and watched as the guard on the first-floor balcony turned his back. She dashed into the bushes at the side of the house while the man was looking away from her. She stopped for a moment to make sure that there were no cries of alarm from any of the remaining guards. Reassured that she had made her approach undetected, she raised her right arm, pointing the grappler unit on her wrist at the roof overhead. She fired the bolt, sending it streaking upward trailing monofilament line until the small green light on her wrist lit up to confirm a solid hit. She hit a button on the grappler and was pulled quickly up onto the roof.

She crept across the red tiles, heading for the rear of the house. Once there, she peeked over the edge, looking at the balcony below, watching the solitary guard walking past beneath her. She waited for a second and then dropped silently to the tiled floor behind him. She took two steps, delivered a swift punch to the back of the man's neck, and lowered his unconscious body gently to the ground. She walked toward the double glass doors halfway down the balcony and then opened them quietly. She slipped inside and closed them behind her. Next she crossed the thick carpeted floor of the room, approaching the enormous mahogany bed, where she looked down at the figure gently snoring beneath the silk sheets. She reached down and gently shook the foot that was sticking out from the bottom of the covers. The man in the bed sat bolt upright, half awake. She was pleased to see his expression change instantly from confusion to stark terror.

"Hello, Carlos," Raven said, drawing the swords from her back.

☻ ☻ ☻

Pietor Furan stared through the toughened glass at the medical lab beyond. On a steel table in the center of the room, a body lay under a white sheet, illuminated by spotlights in the ceiling. He had gone to considerable trouble to acquire the corpse, and he hoped that the other

Disciples would appreciate his efforts. His phone vibrated in his pocket, and he quickly answered it.

"Furan," he said, still staring through the glass.

"Hello, Pietor," the voice on the other end said. "I have bad news."

"I have become rather used to hearing that recently," Furan said. "What is it, Lin Feng?"

"Nero has taken control of the G.L.O.V.E. ruling council. There was nothing I could do to stop it," Lin Feng replied.

"That is unfortunate," Furan said. "It was our hope that you would have already managed to maneuver yourself into that position. That was what you promised us."

"It is impossible," Lin Feng said. "Without Chavez, I do not have enough support on the council to oppose Nero. If Trent had actually managed to eliminate Nero and Darkdoom when he was supposed to, I would have been able to claim the seat at the head of the table, but now—"

"I have just been informed that Señor Chavez met with an unfortunate accident last night," Furan said calmly.

"Raven!" said Lin Feng, sounding shaken. "He was supposed to be protected."

"And he was," Furan replied. "But I trained the girl, and I can tell you that nothing can stop her once she has your scent. Chavez was dead from the moment he initiated his clumsy attack on her."

"What if Nero sends her after me?" Lin Feng asked, sounding panicked.

"Why would he?" Furan asked with a frown.

"Because I told him yesterday that I would not stand for his appointment to the head of the council. I walked out of the meeting."

"That was . . . foolish of you," Furan said. "I suggest that you contact him, apologize profusely for your behavior, and beg for your seat on the council back."

"I cannot do that." Lin Feng sounded indignant. "I have my honor."

"Damn your honor. You will do it, and you will do it now," Furan said angrily, "or you will find out very quickly what happens to people who have outworn their usefulness to us. Raven will be the very least of your worries."

"Very well," Lin Feng said quietly after a moment or two, "but if Nero ever finds out that I am working with you . . ."

"You will die slowly and very, very painfully," Furan said, his voice like ice, "so I suggest that you ensure that never happens. Good-bye, Lin Feng."

Furan snapped the phone shut angrily. He was surrounded by incompetent fools. First Trent and now Lin Feng had failed in his assignment. Furan would have to take charge of the next stage of the Disciples' plan personally.

Beyond the glass a man in a surgical gown had entered the medical lab.

"I am still not sure what purpose this will serve," Dr. Creed said as he walked toward the body on the table.

"Just proceed with the extraction, please, Doctor," Furan replied with a sigh. "We lost all our remaining supply of the Animus fluid when the H.O.P.E. facility was destroyed, and our scans indicate that the fluid within this body remains active. We cannot afford to waste it."

"He's been dead too long," Creed said, shaking his head. "Your scans are mistaken. Animus cannot survive inside a dead host for more than a few hours. Without the body's bioelectric charge—"

"Proceed, Doctor. I will not ask again," Furan said angrily. "Or would you rather I dropped you back into the middle of the rain forest?"

Creed swallowed nervously, turned to the body, and pulled back the sheet.

"Subject Sebastian Trent has been dead for approximately two weeks," the doctor said for the benefit of the cameras recording the procedure. "Cause of death appears to have been either acute Animus poisoning or a double gunshot wound to the heart. Proceeding with the first incision."

Creed started to make the long Y incision that was the first step of any normal autopsy. He recoiled from the body as the thick, oily black fluid seeped from the small cut he had made, and then he frowned as it seemed to pull back inside the body slightly. He leaned closer.

Without warning a thick black tendril snaked out and hit him in the face, oozing around the sides of his surgical mask and flowing into his mouth and nose.

"Get it off me, get it off!" Creed screamed, before his throat was filled with the substance and he dropped to the floor, gurgling and clawing at his face.

"Fascinating," Furan said calmly as Creed thrashed for a moment on the floor and then lay still. If nothing else, Animus might make an effective assassination tool if they were able to replicate more from this small sample. Furan made a mental note that Creed's autopsy would have to be carried out with much more caution. This batch of the fluid seemed uniquely aggressive.

Furan was about to turn away from the glass and summon a cleanup team, when a movement from Creed caught his eye.

Furan watched in amazement as the doctor slowly got back to his feet and staggered toward the glass, placing one hand on it for support. His face was covered in the telltale black traces of Animus poisoning, his eyes closed and his chest rising and falling as he took rapid ragged breaths.

"Are you all right, Doctor?" Furan asked in amazement.

293

No one other than Malpense had ever survived Animus infection before.

"Better than that," Creed said, his eyes flying open and glowing with an inhuman red color.

"I . . . am . . . reborn."